The Navigator's Daughter

A play by
Michael Yates

Nettle Books

Published 2019 by Nettle Books, Yorkshire
nettlebooks@hotmail.com

This volume © 2019 by Michael Yates
ISBN: 978-0-9933729-5-7

Classification: Drama

Dedicated to
Helen Watson,
a great leading lady,
for whom I wrote this play

Cover picture: Keith Pottage as Cyril, Helen Watson as Alice

The original production of *The Navigator's Daughter* took place at Powerhouse One Theatre in Wakefield.

Cast:

Alice...Helen Watson
Maudie.......................................Helen Morris
Tom....................................Andrew Sheppard
Cyril...Keith Pottage
Albert.......................................Simon Bond
Aunt Dot.......................................Janet Rose
Sister.................................Audrey Haggerty
Arthur...,...Ron Hill

Stage Manager Catherine Pidd, Make-up Yvonne Denton, Prompt June Shackleton, Fashion adviser Kirstie Alexander; Technicians: Keith Goodwin, Andy Brown, Susan Easey, Jayne Alexander, Eric Arundell, Tom Dixon, Mollie Dixon, Glenys A Gill, Emilie Wadsworth.

Directed by Alan Alexander

Financially supported by Wakefield District Arts

Cast of characters

ALICE, domineering, promiscuous working class woman, from her attractive late twenties to her senile eighties. There is no apparent ageing during the thirties and forties when passage of time is indicated by change of clothes. But there is a dramatic change in the sixties when her hair is suddenly grey; and after that her deterioration is characterised by her wearing glasses and acting in an increasingly confused and demented fashion. Alice speaks in strong working class Yorkshire vernacular, but it lapses occasionally so we suspect she often "puts it on".

MAUDIE, Alice's intelligent, dowdy daughter, from nine years old – when she still plays with her teddy bear – to her sixties. As an adult, she wears glasses. There is no attempt to portray her switch between adult and child realistically. Although Alice and other characters speak in working class Yorkshire dialect for a good part of the time, Maudie always speaks in standard English – the language she favours as an adult.

DOROTHY, Alice's snobby sister-in-law, from her thirties to her seventies; stupid, amiable.

ALBERT, Alice's brother and Dorothy's husband, in his early thirties, well-meaning but weak and nondescript.

TOM, the first of Alice's lovers, in his twenties, boyish, amiable, ineffectual.

CYRIL, the second of Alice's lovers, in his late thirties, strong, brutal, loud.

HARRY, Alice's American soldier lover, handsome, strong, deceitful.

ARTHUR, the last of Alice's lovers, in his sixties, fat, jovial, stupid.

WARD SISTER at the hospital where Alice is sent; experienced, common-sense sort of woman.

The angry voice of FRANK, Alice's common law husband, is heard but he is never seen.

Setting:

Sheffield, England. Mainly the living room of the house where Alice and Maudie live for 50 years.

Period:

From the 1930s to the 1980s.

ACT I

OPENING MUSIC: HOLDING BACK THE YEARS
BY SIMPLY RED. AS MUSIC FADES, A DJ BEGINS
HIS LINK PATTER AND IS SUDDENLY TURNED
OFF. THE LIGHTS GO UP ON MAUDIE, A SLIGHT
60-YEAR-OLD WOMAN IN SHAPELESS DRESS
AND BI-FOCAL GLASSES. SHE SITS ON A SETTEE
STAGE CENTRE WHICH IS COVERED IN A
"THROW" DECORATED IN A SMART EIGHTIES
PATTERN. MAUDIE, PEN IN HAND, IS DOING A
CROSSWORD PUZZLE OUT OF A NEWSPAPER. A
DICTIONARY SITS ON THE SMALL TABLE TO
HER RIGHT NEXT TO A TELEPHONE. SHE IS
INTENT ON HER TASK AND EVERY SO OFTEN
PUTS THE PAPER DOWN TO CONSULT THE
DICTIONARY. OCCASIONALLY SHE WRITES
DOWN AN ANSWER.

MAUDIE: (READING) A switch in wages is a travesty
of work. (THINKS ABOUT IT, THEN TO
AUDIENCE) Six letters. I've got an R and a D.
(PAUSE) *Pa-ro-dy*. Pay is the wages, rod is the switch.
Yes. (SHE WRITES IT IN) That sort of switch. Not the
electric sort. Not the sort most people would think. (TO
AUDIENCE) I bet you thought electric switch. (PAUSE,
THEN READS) Affection. Devotion. Strong attachment
to the opposite sex. Four letters. That's easy. *Love*.
(BEAT) House. Never away. Four letters. *Home*. That's
easy too. (PAUSES THEN LOOKS UP AT
AUDIENCE) I like crosswords. I'm good at them. I
always was good with words. Now I'm retired, now I've

6

got time on my hands, I like to do the crossword of an evening. It settles me down before bed. (LOOKS DOWN AGAIN) A form of class distinction many children won't wear. Six, seven. *School uniform*. That's easy. (TO AUDIENCE) They always throw in an easy one just to fool you. (SHE WRITES IT IN) *We* wore school uniform. I was good at school. Good at words. Light at the end of the dark. Six. *Tunnel*. That was easy too. (LAUGHS) Maybe it's me. Maybe I'm getting too good. I wouldn't want that. I wouldn't want to be so good that I just finished it in half an hour and then had nothing to do. Well, nothing *interesting*. (PAUSE) There's Cilla Black on the telly but I don't always like it. It's mucky sometimes. The things they say on it, those couples. We never said things like that when I was young. We wouldn't have known the words. And I was good at words. (PAUSE) And she dyes her hair, that Cilla Black. I would never dye mine. There's too many people in this life that dye their hair. It's a form of dishonesty, and I can't stand dishonesty. (WRITES IT IN) *Tunnel*. (LOOKS UP, SUDDENLY EAGER) My grandad built the Woodhead Tunnel. Not on his own. He had lots of other people to help him, that's what Mam always said. He was only small, only a lad. Fetching and carrying for the excavators. (TURNS BACK TO CROSSWORD, READS) Pull in a group is loco. *Steam train*. Team in strain (WRITES IT IN).

LIGHTS GO OFF, RAILWAY SOUNDS, A WHOOSH THROUGH A TUNNEL, THEN THE REGULAR JIGGETY-JIG OF THE TRAIN. LIGHTS GO ON. MAUDIE IS STILL ON THE SETTEE BUT NOW

WRAPPED IN SCARF AND OVERCOAT AND
WITHOUT GLASSES. SHE CARRIES A TEDDY
BEAR. ALICE IS SITTING NEXT TO HER DRESSED
THIRTIES STYLE

ALICE: (POINTING AS IF OUT OF TRAIN
WINDOW): Your grandad was a nipper when they built
that Woodhead Tunnel, Maudie, fetching and carrying
for the excavators. A navvie. A navigator. His dad died
of the cholera with 30 others that was buildin' it and
your grandad was the man of the family then! And he
grew right and strong and he was always the man! Such
a man he was! Oh, it's a shame you never knew 'im! It's a
shame we've only got the photographs! (TURNING TO
MAUDIE) I hope you paid attention. I hope you did,
Maudie. Your grandad was a nipper when they built that
tunnel. (SHE LOOKS OUT OF WINDOW AGAIN) It's
good to be goin' home. (SHE HUGS MAUDIE)

MAUDIE : (TO ALICE) *Are* we goin' home, Mam? Are
we really? Is my dad gonna be there?

ALICE: Nay, lass. Our *real* home, I mean. Where we
come from. Where your Uncle Albert lives. He's got lots
of photos of your grandad.

MAUDIE: I don't remember Uncle Albert. I want to see
my dad.

ALICE: Course you don't remember. You're too young.
Don't you worry about that, our Maudie. You'll see the
photographs

MAUDIE: (TO AUDIENCE) Of course I don't remember. Of course I'm too young. I'm only nine and I'm still playing with teddy bears. I don't remember my grandad and I don't remember my Uncle Albert. But I remember my dad. Oh, dad! Dad! (LIGHTS OFF)

VOICE OF MAUDIE'S DAD: (SHOUTING) What do you mean by it? What do you bloody mean? I treated you right, didn't I? I stood by you when others wouldn't! An' you shat on me, that's a fact! What a fool I've been, what a bloody fool! What a dance you've led me! An' I don't suppose it's the first time...!

SPOTLIGHT ON ALICE, STANDING FRONT OF STAGE, GAZING OUT AGGRESSIVELY AT THE AUDIENCE

ALICE: (IN A CALM VOICE) Nay, and it won't be the last! Treated me right, did tha? Tha's not treated us like a man'ud treat us! Tha's not a man! Tha can't keep thy women! Led you a dance, did I? Make a song and dance about it. (STARTS TO SING) Oooh-oooh, da-dee-dah-dee-dah and heaven was in your eyes, the night that I told you those little white lies... (SHE LAUGHS CONTEMPTUOUSLY)

VOICE OF MAUDIE'S DAD: If you go through that door, you needn't look to come back! You nor the lass! I'm warning you, Alice!

ALICE: Warnin' *me*!

SHE LAUGHS AGAIN. INTO THE SPOTLIGHT
WALKS MAUDIE, STILL IN SCARF AND
OVERCOAT AND WITHOUT GLASSES,
CARRYING HER TEDDY BEAR. ALICE TAKES
MAUDIE BY THE HAND AND PICKS UP A
SUITCASE AND THEY BEGIN WALKING ON THE
SPOT

ALICE: *Him* warning *me*! Did you ever hear of such a
thing? (SHE BEGINS TO SING UNDER HER
BREATH) Ooooh, love me or leave me, de-da-dum. de-
only, da-dum-dee-da-dum, and never be lonely... (SHE
LAUGHS AGAIN, PUTS DOWN THE SUITCASE,
TAKES HOLD OF MAUDIE) Now, it's thee an' me, the
two of us, now and always, does tha understand? (SHE
TICKLES MAUDIE WHO BEGINS TO LAUGH) We'll
be seeing your uncle Albert right soon. You've not seen
him since you were small.

MAUDIE: (GIGGLING) Stop it! Stop it!

ALICE: (STILL TICKLING HER) Round and round the
garden, like a teddy bear. Tickle, tickle! You know you
love it, Maudie. You know you do!

MAUDIE DROPS HER TEDDY, BREAKS AWAY,
LAUGHING, AND THE SPOTLIGHT FOLLOWS
HER AS SHE FALLS ON THE SETTEE, LEAVING
THE REST OF THE STAGE IN DARKNESS

MAUDIE: *Tickle*. Six letters. (SHE TAKES OFF HER OVERCOAT AND SCARF, PUTS ON HER GLASSES, PICKS UP THE DICTIONARY, FLIPS THROUGH IT AND READS) To excite. To disturb with a light touch, usually uncomfortable. (CLOSES IT). I've always hated it, always hated being tickled. Why don't people listen? Why don't people believe you? Ever since I was small...

VOICE OF ALICE: (WEARY AND AGITATED) Ever since you were small! It's been thee and me, the two of us. You know how much I love my home. *Our* home. I do. I don't like bein' away. I don't like being 'ere! In this bed. In this 'ospital. I don't! Take me home, Maudie!

THE TELEPHONE RINGS

MAUDIE: (PICKS UP THE PHONE) Hello, Dot. That's right. I've seen the doctor. I've seen the sister on the ward. I've seen everybody. Well, you know what she's like. I know what I'm doing, Dot. She *is* my mother! I told them I don't expect miracles. (REPEATS IN LOUDER VOICE) *Miracles*. Eight letters. Supernatural events. Marvels. Wonders. (SLAMS DOWN THE PHONE)

LIGHTS GO UP ACROSS THE STAGE. A NURSE SITS AT A DESK. THERE IS ANOTHER CHAIR IN FRONT OF IT. MAUDIE GOES ACROSS TO HER

MAUDIE: (SITTING DOWN) I said I don't expect miracles. But you'll have to tell me straight – how long has she got?

SISTER: No, no, that's not what I mean. Not what I mean at all. She could go on for years. I just mean she'll not get better. She'll have times like today when she's not too poorly, when she knows you and talks to you and remembers things and makes sense. Periods of remission, we call them. But they'll get shorter, less frequent... And the other times... (SHE GLANCES AT A REPORT ON HER DESK) The shaking and trembling, the falling down, messing herself, forgetting what you've told her two minutes ago, telling lies, obsessive behaviour...

MAUDIE: First it was sweets and cakes and things. I'd come home and find the drawers full of barley sugars and chocolate buttons. Like a kid, she was. I didn't know whether to laugh or cry. And now she washes her hair five, six times a day when she's at home. I hide the shampoo but she uses Fairy Liquid...

SISTER: We'll give you some tablets for the trembling so she should be able to feed herself, and some for the bowels and some others to make her sleep. Now, has anybody spoken to you about attendance allowance?

MAUDIE: (TO AUDIENCE) Tablets. Seven letters. Pills of stone. *Tablets*. Pills. I've started taking pills. Not a lot. Just a few. (BEAT) We've always managed before. We've both got our pensions and there's no rent or...

(BEAT, THEN TO SISTER) You mean she's coming home again? Permanent?

SISTER: There's nothing more we can do. And there are so many people these days, we just don't have the beds. The only alternative, you realise, is some kind of... institution...

MAUDIE: Oh no, no. I'd never do that. She's my mother. I couldn't put her away.

SISTER: Now – this attendance allowance. It's not like winning the Pools, but it's not to be sniffed at. And she wants to go home, talks about nothing else. And it might do some good, you never can tell. Oh, she wants to go home allright, drives us batty with it...

MAUDIE GETS UP AND IS SPOTLIGHTED AS LIGHTS GO DOWN ON SISTER AND DESK

MAUDIE: *Home.* Four letters. Never away. We didn't always have a home...

LIGHT GOES UP IN DIFFERENT PART OF STAGE TO REVEAL POTTED PLANTS AND PIANO WITH A NUMBER OF PHOTOGRAPHS RANGED ON TOP. ALICE STANDS IMPATIENTLY HOLDING MAUDIE'S TEDDY BEAR. THE SUITCASE IS ON THE FLOOR

ALICE: Come on, Maudie! Don't leave me holdin' Pooh.

13

MAUDIE: (PUTS GLASSES IN POCKET, RUNS UP AND TAKES TEDDY FROM ALICE) It's nice, mam. It's got a piano. It's got flowers. Is this our new home?

ALICE: (CONTEMPTUOUSLY) It's a conservatory, Maudie. Happen tha's not seen a conservatory before. It's where they like to put their piano. *Grandad's* piano. Out of the way. These photos must be Dorothy's. Well, they're not Albert's. It's a conservatory, Maudie. It's where they ask their visitors to wait.

MAUDIE: Is this our new home?

ALICE: No, love. But it's the home of them as owes us summat.

MAUDIE: I want to go home! You promised!

ALICE: (PULLING AWAY FROM HER) I've got just the song for you, lass. You know you like a song, you like to hear your mam sing. (SHE WALKS JAUNTILY ACROSS TO THE PIANO, OPENS THE STOOL, BEGINS TO LEAF THROUGH SOME SHEET MUSIC, HUMS AND SINGS) Don't let it bother you when skies are grey, la-di-da,la-di-da, everything will be OK... I'll work for you, I'll slave for you, I'll be a beggar or a knave for you, and if that isn't love, it will have to do, until the real thing comes along... (STOPS SINGING) Here it is. The real thing. (SHE FINDS THE MUSIC, SITS DOWN AND STARTS PLAYING AND SINGING)   Ooooh, shoooow me the way to go home,

14

I'm tired and I wanna go to bed, I had a little drink about an hour ago and it's gone right to my head...

SHE STOPS AND LOOKS ACROSS THE ROOM AS ALBERT ENTERS

ALBERT: I'm sorry I've kept you waiting. I'm doing all I can.

ALICE: I don't know that one. Have you got the Al Bowlly version? (PAUSE)) It's that Dorothy, that bloody wife o' thine! With her airs and graces an' her bloody piano! *Our* bloody piano! She's turned thee against us!

ALBERT: Nay, nay. You don't understand!

ALICE: You've got a nice home, Albert. And a nice conservatory. Maudie thinks so. Are these your songs then? (LEAFING THROUGH SHEET MUSIC) Your favourites? Or are they Dorothy's? Come on, I'll sing you a song. Any song you want. That's what you sing to her, isn't it? Any song she bloody wants.

ALBERT: She's my wife.

ALICE: And I'm only tha sister. Come on, Albert. You've got some good ones. (SHE SIFTS THROUGH THE MUSIC) Careless Love, There'll Be Some Changes Made, Someone to Watch Over Me...

ALBERT: (IN NERVOUS WHISPER) You know what the trouble is. If thee an' that Frank had done right an' proper thing before the bairn came along...

ALICE: (RAISING HER VOICE) If we'd got wed, like you and Dorothy got wed, we'd be respectable. I know. Still, she never liked us, that Dorothy. I suppose when you marry brass, you've got to expect a bit o' tarnish.

ALBERT: It's not that. It's not Dorothy. It's just... I've a good position now, and with our own bairn on the way...

ALICE: If our dad could hear thee now, God rest 'im, he'd take his belt to thee!

ALBERT: Don't go on about our dad!

ALICE: He looked after us when Mam died. And he never brought another woman back. It was him and thee and me, the three of us. Family.

ALBERT: We're still family...

ALICE: I wonder what he'd think of you now. His little man, he used to call you. Well, little is true enough. Nay, I don't suppose it does much for thy position in life, having a dad that was a common navvy. Well, we had a piano once, I'll thank you to remember. I've still got it in the photos, so I can prove who it belongs to, see if I can't. I look at us how we was then an' I think...

ALBERT: (PLACATING HER) Look, look... (HE PUTS AN ARM ROUND HER SHOULDERS BUT SHE BACKS AWAY, THROWING THE MUSIC SHEETS ACROSS THE ROOM. MAUDIE, EXCITED, CATCHES SOME OF THE SHEETS AND SQUEALS AND LAUGHS)

ALBERT: Look - there's no room here, not with the bairn on the way. Tha can see for thyssen.

ALICE: I wasn't thinking of sleeping in the conservatory.

ALBERT: Well, there is... there is an *'ouse.*

ALICE: I don't suppose *that's* got a conservatory.

ALBERT: It's got a kitchen and a parlour and two rooms above. There's many would be satisfied with that. *Should* be satisfied.

ALICE: Where?

ALBERT: The Wicker. Near the station. Oh, I don't say it's much, but it's summat... It's one of a pair that Dorothy's dad had give him by way of settlement for a debt. We don't expect rent, mind, not till you get on your feet again.

ALICE: That's how some make their money, isn't it? Getting other folk into debt. So that's what you've married into. Well, don't worry. You'll get what's due when I've got it to give. (SHE HUGS MAUDIE AND KISSES HER) Little Maudie an' me pay us way, don't we, duck?

ALBERT: (WRINGING HIS HANDS) Oh, Alice... Why'd you leave him, lass? We'd hoped, Dorothy and me, that it'd all work out in the end. He seemed a nice enough lad, did Frank.

ALICE: The world's full of nice lads. It's *men* that's scarce. Men that'll stick by thee an' not wittle on about their position.

ALBERT: You'll be needing some brass to tide you over, I dare say. I've got something here... (HANDS OVER TWO TEN SHILLING NOTES) Look, it's not a bad house, you know. (TO MAUDIE) You'll like it, Maudie. It's got little angels carved in the corners of the ceiling in the parlour. Little cherr-abims. Lovely little angels...

ALICE: They'll be the only angels we'll ever see then. The world's not good enough for angels, Maudie, and you shouldn't go thinking it is. Else you *will* be disappointed.

MAUDIE: I like angels. I like their wings.

ALICE: (TO ALBERT): It's fairies she's thinking of. Fairies on Christmas trees. She's never seen angels.

ALBERT: There's angels on Christmas trees too. Anyway, where's the difference?

ALICE: Ay, it's only with *people* that you've got to worry about the differences, Maudie. Who's your friend and who isn't. Who bothers about thee and who doesn't. You've got to choose the right ones to depend on.

ALBERT: That's not fair. You can depend on us. You always could.

ALICE: For a slum on The Wicker and two ten bob notes? So your new friends up Hallam way won't get wind of us, your little family secret? Ta very much. Pity I couldn't choose my brother, Maudie.

ALBERT: That's a terrible thing to say. You expect too much.

ALICE: I always have. It's a fault of mine. And so does Maudie. And she's got a right to expect things. (PAUSE) Now, what I really fancied was a piano. Like we used to have. Like our dad bought. (STROKES THE PIANO) Like this one. And a room big enough for one. Still, angels on the ceiling, Maudie, watching over you. (SINGS) There's a somebody I'm longing to see, I hope that he turns out to be... an *angel* to watch over me.

THE LIGHT GOES UP ON THE SETTEE. MAUDIE WALKS SWIFTLY OVER TO IT, THROWS DOWN THE TEDDY, PUTS ON HER GLASSES, PICKS UP THE DICTIONARY AND THUMBS THROUGH IT. THE LIGHTS GO DOWN ON THE REST OF THE STAGE

MAUDIE: (TO THE AUDIENCE) *Angel*. Five letters.
Divine messenger. A dead person received into heaven.
(LOOKS THROUGH DICTIONARY AGAIN) *Fairy*.
Five letters. An imaginary being, of diminutive form,
capable of kind acts, but sometimes bad or mischievous.
(PAUSES, PICKS UP THE PAPER, READS
ANOTHER CLUE) Obscure experience. Not far ahead.
But isn't a draughty place. Eight, five. Anagram. It's got
to be an anagram. I've got the D. It is. It's an anagram.
Isn't a draughty. The five-letter word will be...
Day...Days...Nights...Night. It's night. It's night. It's
Saturday night. I've got it. It's Saturday night. And you
don't have to go out on a Saturday night. Not when
you've got a home. Home. Four letters. Never away.
(PAUSE) And we came home and it wasn't much. Like
Uncle Albert said. But it was home. And Uncle Albert
bought us things. He came round and brought us things.
A little table. A couple of chairs. He brought *me* things.
Presents. Dolls. Sweets. Children's things. Girls' things.

MAUDIE TAKES OFF HER GLASSES, STARTS TO
LICK A LOLLY, ALICE COMES INTO THE LIGHT
AND SITS NEXT TO MAUDIE

ALICE: I'll thank that uncle of thine, my good brother,
not to treat us like a bloody charity case. Thee should
learn to say no, Maudie. Tha needs a bit o' pride. Tha's
not too young to know that. Tha doesn't get anywhere
with men by saying yes all the time. They bring thee all
the cheap stuff and think that's all tha's worth. Look at
what Albert brings thee – rag dolls, gobstoppers... When

I was same age as thee, our dad brought us real toys, real things, things he'd made himself, dolls carved out of wood, train engines and animals carved the same. And when he brought us sweets, he brought us sweets in tins and boxes lined with silver paper, humbugs and caramel toffee, not ha' penny lollies that you stick in your pocket and get all fluff on. And they're bad for thy teeth, them cheap sweets. (SHE SNATCHES LOLLY AWAY)

MAUDIE: (INDIGNANT) I *like* lollies. I like Uncle Albert. You're not nice to him.

ALICE: A girl like thee is too young to know what's nice. He only comes round here because they lost the son and heir.

MAUDIE: What do you mean?

ALICE: Tha'll understand when tha's older.

MAUDIE: Is it Auntie Dorothy? Is it because she didn't have her baby?

ALICE: Aunty Dot had a bit of trouble...

MAUDIE: And the baby died before it could be born. He's gone to heaven to be an angel. Like the ones on the ceiling. That's what Uncle Albert told me.

ALICE: Well, there's some things he shouldn't be saying to a girl of your age. But it's true enough. And she'll never have a baby now. Not with what the doctors did to her. That's why Albert takes an interest these days. We're his only kin, thee and me, Maudie. It's punishment. That's what I tell him. And he's got to make it up to us if he wants forgiveness.

MAUDIE: Do you think God will forgive him then?

ALICE: God? Nay, it's not God he needs to forgive him, it's me. If it were God, he'd be off the hook by now. That's because God's a man. But I'm not so easy to get on with. (BEAT) Anyway, he's come through with a bit of stuff and it's a bit more like home now. Though I begrudge that piano. It's half mine, (HUGS MAUDIE) half *ours*. That's what our dad would have wanted. Not given up to some pawnbroker's daughter that can't play Chopsticks. Today it's stuck in the conservatory, next week it'll be out in the garden. (BEAT) Still, we've got some bits of stuff and we've got Tom now. And he's a help round the house if nothing else. (SHE HUGS MAUDIE)

MUSIC: UNTIL THE REAL THING COMES ALONG BY FATS WALLER. AS MUSIC FADES, THE LIGHTS GO UP ON THE WHOLE STAGE AND WE SEE FOR THE FIRST TIME THE LIVING ROOM OF THE HOUSE. THERE IS A SMALL WOODEN TABLE COVERED IN A CHEAP TABLECLOTH WITH CUPS AND SAUCERS ON IT AND A RICKETY OLD EASY CHAIR IN WHICH A MAN SITS. THERE IS A PEG RUG ON THE FLOOR

MAUDIE: I like Tom. Are you going to be nice to him?

ALICE: Well, don't go liking him *too* much. (SHOUTS ACROSS TO THE MAN IN THE CHAIR) Tom, I've got a job for thee. There's water coming into the cellar.

TOM: Water in the cellar. O'course there's water in the cellar. That's what cellars are for. It's when you get it up to the floorboards that you start worrying, woman.

ALICE: (GOING OVER TO HIM) It's making the coal wet. So don't give me none of your lip, Tom. Not that kind, anyway. (SHE KISSES HIM LONG AND LINGERING)

MAUDIE: (TO AUDIENCE) I like Tom. He's a bit like dad. But I can't say why. Anyway, he's kind to me like Mam. *Kind*. Four letters. Demonstrating charity or of the same family. I like the house too. Home. Only we didn't have the phone then and we didn't have such a nice settee. (SHE STANDS UP, PULLS THE "THROW" OFF THE SETTEE, REVEALING IT AS OLD AND DECREPIT. SHE PUTS THE THROW OVER THE TELEPHONE)

TOM: (COMING ACROSS TO MAUDIE) I've kissed tha mam and now I'll kiss thee. (HE KISSES AND HUGS HER, PICKS HER UP AND WHIRLS HER ROUND; THE EFFECT IS INNOCENT AND PLAYFUL) See those little angels? See those little angels up ont' ceiling? They're like thee, Maudie. Thee's my little angel! (HE DROPS HER ON THE SETTEE. SHE LAUGHS AND PICKS UP HER EXERCISE

BOOK AND PENCIL WHICH WERE UNDER THE
THROW)

ALICE: (OBVIOUSLY ANNOYED AS SHE MAKES
MOUTHS IN AN IMAGINARY MIRROR AND
ADJUSTS HER MAKEUP) Leave the girl alone. Leave
Maudie alone.

TOM: Jealous? (HE GOES OVER TO ALICE AND
PUTS HIS ARMS AROUND HER) Tha's no need to be.
Maudie's my little angel, but thee's ma big 'un! Thee's a
beauty! (HE KISSES HER NECK)

ALICE : (SHRUGGING HIM OFF WITH A SHOW OF
ANGER BUT OBVIOUSLY ENJOYING HIS
ATTENTIONS) None o' thy sauce! Oh, now tha's
smudged us! (SHE SLAPS HIS HAND AND RE-
TOUCHES HER MAKE-UP)

TOM: (BLOWING ON HIS HAND AND DANCING
ROUND THE ROOM IN A JOKY PANTOMIME
WHICH AMUSES MAUDIE) Oh, oh, the pain! The
pain! I don't know what I'll do! Oh, tha's done for me,
Alice! (HE WINKS AT MAUDIE)

ALICE: (REALLY ANGRY NOW) Tha's a babby! An'
tha'll always be a babby! Now stop laykin' about for a
minute!

MAUDIE: (PORING OVER HER EXERCISE BOOKS
THEN TURNING TO TOM AS HE SETTLES IN THE

CHAIR OPPOSITE) How d'you turn fractions into decimals, Uncle Tom?

TOM: Oh dear. That's summat they don't teach us ont' coalface. We've no need of it. Can't do sums int' dark. Now I'm a grafter down there, by God I am, but yer mam makes us work a damn sight harder up here an' no mistake! (HE LEANS ACROSS TO HER IN MOCK SECRECY) Let's just see what I've gone an' done this morning to earn me bit o' Sunday rest. (HE PICKS OUT OF HIS POCKET A PACKET OF WOODBINES AND A BOX OF SWAN VESTAS AND GLANCES SURREPTITIOUSLY OVER AT ALICE STILL BY THE MIRROR TO MAKE SURE SHE IS STILL LISTENING) I've cleaned the grate, I've scrubbed the kitchen floor and put newspaper down. I've cut up the *Mail* an' hung it int' privy out back, (MAUDIE GIGGLES AT THIS) I've rubbed us shoes wi' lard to make 'em shine an' squeal like new, good enough to go to church in, though the only place yer mam wants to go on Sunday is the pub. Laykin', she says! (HE LIGHTS A CIGARETTE AND LOOKS ROUND FOR SOMEWHERE TO DROP THE MATCH; IN THE END, HE PUTS IT BACK IN THE BOX) Don't want to burn your mam's rug. I don't think she's noticed, preenin' herself in front o' glass. Tha wouldn't tell on me if I did, would tha, Maudie? Tha wouldn't tell 'er what I done?

MAUDIE : (GIGGLING) You know I wouldn't.

TOM: Ay, I *do*. I know tha's straight an' wouldn't give us away. An' I know tha's clever too.

ALICE: (STILL FACING MIRROR) Don't think I don't know what goes on. (SHE TURNS AND FACES THEM) How do I look, Tom Dutton? Here, give us a puff. Tha's good for buyin' us Woodbines if nowt else.

TOM: (HANDING HER CIGARETTE) You look like a film star.

MAUDIE: You look like that Marlene Dietrich, mam.

TOM: Even better. More life-like.

ALICE: (BRIGHTENING, OBVIOUSLY PLEASED) More life-like than *thee*, Tom Dutton. Half the time. Well, stir thyssen or we'll miss the bus. It's always the same, gabbin' with our Maudie, tellin' her she's clever. It won't do her no good, turnin' her head like that. She'll just go on sittin' on her backside all day writin' things.

MAUDIE: (LOOKING GUILTY) It's for school, mam.

ALICE: (POSING WITH CIGARETTE) You'll need glasses soon and then where'll you be? You're no beauty queen now. You'll end up wi' some man wi' no more gumption than your Uncle Tom, and that's nowt to look forward to.

MAUDIE: I like you, Tom.

TOM: Ta, Maudie. She doesn't allus do sums, you know, Alice? She writes poetry, don't you, lass?

MAUDIE : (SHOOTING TOM AN ANGRY GLANCE) Only for school.

ALICE: You do too much for school. (SHE GIVES TOM THE CIGARETTE BACK) Oh, I know who gives you grand ideas – if it's not Tom, it's your Aunt Dorothy. I've never liked that woman and she don't like us. The only reason she's taken to thee is she's got no bairns of her own.

MAUDIE: (UPSET) Oh, mam...

ALICE: Tha knows I say these things for thy own good, duck. Now, there's plenty o' tea an' some fresh cheese int' pantry an' some o' them arrowroot biscuits you're partial to. See, I look after thee, Maudie. Gi' us a kiss then.

MAUDIE HUGS AND KISSES ALICE AND TOM. TOM PICKS UP HIS JACKET AND CAP FROM THE TABLE AND HE AND ALICE GO OUT AT THE BACK, STAGE RIGHT. MAUDIE CONTINUES TO WRITE IN HER EXERCISE BOOKS. AFTER A BIT, SHE TAKES A BOOK FROM THE BOTTOM OF THE PILE AND OPENS IT

MAUDIE: (IN A SELF-CONSCIOUS READING ALOUD STYLE OF VOICE) The World is a Star, by Maude Corner, Aged 11. (COUGHS) The world is a star, / Seen by other stars, / Aglow with itself / And the people on it. / The world is a star, / But I only see / The light of other stars / Falling on me. / The world is a star, /

Brilliant in space, / Beautiful to watch / From some other place.

MAUDIE: (TO AUDIENCE) I got an A-plus and a star for that one. Miss Appleby said it was really good. She says she likes my poems and I ought to write more. She says I'm good with words.

(READS AGAIN) The Centre of the World. / I am the centre of the world./ I look out from inside me./ And we and you and they are the centres of the world./ They look out at me./ So many centres, so many worlds, / So many people./ But only you for me, only you./ Be the centre of my world. (SHE HUGS THE BOOK TO HER) I didn't show that one to Miss Appleby. She'd make me read it out in class and I couldn't do that. The other girls would ask me what it meant and I couldn't tell them. Or they'd say it was about love and boys and things. And they'd laugh. But when I'm on my own, when Tom and mam are out, then I like to read it. I don't need to get A-plus because I know it's good. I'm good with words.

SHE LIES DOWN ACROSS THE SETTEE AND CLOSES HER EYES. THE LIGHTS DIM AT THE BACK, LEAVING ONLY THE SETTEE LIT UP. AFTER A WHILE TOM AND ALICE ENTER AT THE BACK, STAGE RIGHT

TOM: I can't find light switch. Wait. Hang on. I've got it. (LIGHTS GO ON)

ALICE: Give us back me key. (PAUSE, THEN ANGRILY) You should've stood up to 'im!

TOM: Don't take on.

ALICE: Is that all tha thinks of me? Is that how little tha feels for me? That a fella like that can say what he said...

TOM: He's my mate.

ALICE: That makes it allright then, does it?

TOM: He didn't say owt.

ALICE: Going on about my legs.

TOM: He didn't mean owt. I don't know what tha's going on about.

ALICE: Didn't *mean* owt! I know what he meant. Everybody in the pub knew what he meant. I've never been so shamed!

TOM: He didn't mean owt. He'd had a drop too much. All he said...

ALICE: Made me out to be cheap, some tart...

TOM: He didn't say that. I'd've clouted him if he'd said anything bad. But he didn't.

ALICE: He said I looked like one.

TOM: *The Blue Angel*. He said you looked like the Blue Angel. In the film.

ALICE: Well, we know what kind of film that is. We don't have to see it to know what kind of film that is.

TOM: He meant tha looked like a film star.

ALICE: He talked about my legs.

TOM: He didn't mean owt.

ALICE: Men don't talk about women's legs in public. It's not decent. Not in front of the woman. Not in front of me.

TOM: He's a mate of mine. He works on my shift.

ALICE: Oh, well, then it's allright, if he's a mate of thine, if he works on same shift. I know it's a right mucky place down the pit, but that doesn't mean he can bring his dirt up here.

TOM: He didn't mean owt. Honest he didn't. I know him. I don't know why tha's taking on so. Look, I'll talk to 'im. When I see him.

ALICE: *Talk to 'im*, is it? Oh, that'll be nice. Thee and the lads can have a little chat about me when you're on t'coalface together. You probably do anyway. You're a right bunch of bastards.

TOM: (EMBARRASSED) Don't say things like that. I don't like to hear strong language from thee, Alice. Tha's being daft about it.

ALICE: I'm daft now, am I? Oh yes, that'll be where the lads all talk about their women.

TOM: That's daft. Stop it. I don't know why...

ALICE: Some men wouldn't let their mates talk that way. Some men wouldn't just have a *talk* with their mates. Some men would show their mates what's what. But maybe he's a bit closer than a mate. Maybe he were jealous tonight. Maybe talk isn't all you lads get up to down there.

TOM: I don't know why it's made thee upset...

ALICE: *Talk to 'im. Talk to 'im.* Well, some men, *real* men wouldn't stop at a talking-to. Some men would give 'im a fist. Like this.

SHE PUNCHES TOM WHO ROCKS BACK ON HIS HEELS, OBVIOUSLY HURT, AND MAKES AS THOUGH TO HIT HER BACK

TOM: (ANGRY) You... you...!

ALICE: Go on then. Tha doesn't want to hit thy precious mate, so why doesn't tha hit me?

TOM: (RESTRAINING HIMSELF) Tha's gone daft. Tha's gone funny in the head. I can't make thee out. (HE TURNS AWAY, UPSET, WANDERS IN FRONT OF THE SETTEE, SEES MAUDIE WHO HAS COME AWAKE) Maudie!

ALICE: (ANGRILY TO MAUDIE) Maudie! What does tha think tha's doing down here at this time? Thee should be in bed, my girl. I told thee we'd be late. I told thee to look after thyssen.

MAUDIE : (UPSET) I fell asleep.

ALICE: Fell asleep! I don't like thee listening in on Tom and me. It's none of thy business! (GRABS HOLD OF EXERCISE BOOK) Fell asleep! I'm not surprised. Tha doesn't get proper rest.

MAUDIE: (GRABBING THE BOOK BACK) I'm sorry. I didn't mean to listen.

TOM: Don't fret, lass. It were nothing. Just a bit of a barney. It's soon over.

ALICE: (TO TOM) That's for *me* to decide.

TOM: It were nothing. Nothing for a little'un like Maudie to worry about.

ALICE: Oh, I don't know. Now that she's heard the first bit, maybe she should stay up and hear the rest.

TOM: Stop it, Alice!

ALICE: After all, she'll be looking out for a man herself some day. And she'll want to know the things to look for, the things a *woman* looks for.

TOM: I said to stop it.

ALICE: *You* said? *You* said stop it? She'll not want to get off with a wrong'un. She'll not want to get off with some man who'll not stick up for her...

TOM: Stop it!

ALICE: ...Some man who'll turn tail when there's a real man around...

TOM: Stop!

ALICE: (TO MAUDIE) Did he say something? What did he say, Maudie? Did our Tom say something? Because I'm having trouble with my hearing lately. And I can't hear what Tom says any more. I just can't hear...

TOM: Stop! (HE SLAPS HER AND SHE FALLS BACK ON THE SETTEE)

TOM: (BACKING AWAY IN HORROR) I don't...I don't understand... Oh God! I'm sorry, Alice, I'm sorry, Maudie! I didn't mean...

ALICE: (GETTING UP AND SMOOTHING HER SKIRT) That's allright, Tom. I asked for it. (SHE GOES TO THE MIRROR AND LOOKS AT HER FACE) Wouldn't be surprised if it didn't come up a real shiner in the morning. Tha's got quite a wallop there, Tom. When tha's bothered to use it. (SHE COMES OVER TO HIM AND CUPS HIS FACE IN HER HANDS) Now go up to bed and I'll come up after thee, allright? When I've seen Missie here tucked up.

TOM: (STILL SHOCKED BY WHAT HAS HAPPENED) I'm sorry. I...

ALICE: (SEDUCTIVELY) It's up to thee to make it up to me, isn't it? Go on now. I won't be long.

TOM LEAVES, STAGE LEFT, STILL SHAKING

ALICE: (TO MAUDIE) Well, lass, there's something new for thee to put in them poems now.

MAUDIE: (SHOCKED) Oh, mam! Why...

ALICE: What's the point in having a man for doing the housework? Where's the good in that? If a woman can't keep *house*, she'll not keep anything. And if a *man* keeps house, it's a good bet the woman's keeping something else on the quiet. What's the good in saying sorry and holding thy tongue and keeping all of it inside thyssen instead of letting it out? Life's not like poems, Maudie. Poems are quiet. Life's loud. Life's *songs*, not poems.

Life's singing and dancing and making a noise. Tom can't dance and he doesn't sing much either.

MAUDIE: He's nice.

ALICE: Course he's nice. And he'll be real nice to me tonight. He'll have to say sorry again. Now there's a good time to say sorry – when tha's really done summat. *Sorry I belted thee, Alice.* Not (SHE PUTS ON A COMIC UPPER CLASS ACCENT) *Sorry for bothering you, old gel, can you pass the salt?* When you're both upset, then the two of you can make up. No point making up if you've not had a bit of a barney first.

MAUDIE: Tom *is* going to stay, isn't he?

ALICE: Get some sleep, girl. Don't go worrying thyssen about grown-up things! (SHE LOOKS OVER HER SHOULDER) God, we haven't got much, have we? But we'll get more. See if we don't.

THEY EXIT. LIGHTS DIM. MUSIC: THESE FOOLISH THINGS BY BILLIE HOLIDAY. AS LIGHTS GO ON AGAIN, MAUDIE IN HER NIGHTDRESS LIES ON SETTEE CRAYONING IN A BOOK, ALICE IS IN THE CHAIR, LISTENING TO THE RADIO. ENTER CYRIL AT BACK, STAGE RIGHT

CYRIL: (SHOUTING TO UNSEEN FRIENDS AT THE FRONT DOOR) I'll see thee then. Ay, it were a reet good neet! Expensive for some, maybe. Unlucky for some. But we all get a run of bad luck now and again and all we can do is 'ave a little patience and grit us teeth while it ends. Alice! Maudie! Say goodnight to me pals – they're just off!

ALICE: (TURNS OFF MUSIC ON RADIO, GOES OVER TO THE DOOR, SHOUTS OUT) G'night, Charlie. G'night, Sam. (TO CYRIL AS HE COMES INTO THE ROOM) You should've brought them in, Cyril. I'd've made 'em a cup of tea.

CYRIL: Nay, lass. They're not in the mood. And neither am I – not for a cup of tea anyway. (SHOUTS) Twenty-five pound! Twenty-five pound in a night! Hah! Bloody fools! (HE GUFFAWS, TAKES A PACK OF CARDS FROM HIS POCKET AND THROWS THEM ALL OVER THE ROOM, THEN DOES A LITTLE JIG. ALICE LAUGHS, MAUDIE LOOKS UP FROM WHERE SHE'S LYING ON THE FLOOR, COLOURING IN HER BOOK) Come on, Alice girl! Bring out a bottle! We've got summat to celebrate an' we can afford it tonight!

ALICE: I don't know we've got owt.

CYRIL: You've always got something. Have a look in the kitchen, under the sink. Tha's always got summat stashed away, even when *I've* not, I know tha does…

ALICE: Pick up those cards, Maudie. Pick them up for your Uncle Cyril. There's a good girl. (SHE GOES OFF STAGE LEFT INTO KITCHEN)

CYRIL: Ay, pick up the cards, Maudie. Pick up the lucky cards. (HE WATCHES HER AS SHE RUSHES ABOUT DOING SO) Tell us again how old thee is, Maudie. Thirteen, is it? Still believe in Father Christmas, then? Still believe in fairy tales? Well, I'm Father Christmas tonight, my angel, I'm the good fairy godfather, that's me. (ALICE RETURNS WITH A BOTTLE OF WHISKY AND TWO GLASSES AND PUTS THEM ON THE TABLE) Here, Alice, love, touch the cards, lass, feel them cards. Lucky cards. (AS MAUDIE GIVES THEM TO HIM, HE OFFERS THEM TO ALICE AND RUBS THEM SLOWLY AGAINST HER FACE, SEDUCTIVELY) These little cards have worked a treat tonight, so they have. Come on, Alice. Touch them for luck. The whole pack. Here. Touch. Touch it, Alice. Touch it for the good luck it brings. (SHE DOES SO, EXCITEDLY) You too, Maudie. Touch it for luck. (MAUDIE APPROACHES HIM RELUCTANTLY HOLDS OUT HER HAND AND TOUCHES THE PACK WITH HER FINGERTIPS, LIGHTLY, NERVOUSLY. SUDDENLY CYRIL REACHES FORWARD WITH HIS FREE HAND AND ENCLOSES HERS) Come on, Maudie! Ay up. It won't bite, tha knows. It's good, it's nice. Nice pack o'cards, nice to us tonight. Go on. Touch it proper. (SUDDENLY HIS MOOD CHANGES, HIS VOICE BECOMES ANGRY) Touch it like you'd touch a lad you was courting, all soft an' loving an' gentle like. Else you know what you'll get.

ALICE: (SHE PULLS AWAY, ANGRILY) I won't have talk like that. Not with a lass her age. It's not right.

CYRIL: (LAUGHING) Gerraway! She'll be left school next year, but she's not too old for me to chastise 'er. An' neither is *thee*!

ALICE: (TO MAUDIE) Go on. Go on, Maudie. Do as Uncle Cyril says. For your mam's sake, eh?

MAUDIE TOUCHES THE PACK AGAIN, SLOWLY THIS TIME, BRUSHING THE SURFACE WITH ALL HER FINGERS

CYRIL: (LAUGHING, EXCITED) Shouldn't wonder if tha's not got a lad already.

MAUDIE: I haven't. (TO ALICE) Honest.

ALICE: Course not. Thee and me's got no secrets, have we, duck? (SHE CARRIES THE BOTTLE ACROSS TO THE TABLE)

CYRIL: Only two glasses, Alice? Bring us another. We're family, aren't we? We're family now. My luck is thy luck and Maudie's too. We're all going to share in my luck, all of us. We're going to celebrate it proper.

ALICE: I'll not have you start my daughter off on strong drink, Cyril Cottingham. Anyway, it's well past her bedtime. It's past *our* bedtime for that matter. I only kept

Maudie up for company because I didn't have thee back home.

CYRIL: Bedtime? What's this about bedtime? Eh, come on, Alice, it's a special night! (HE GRABS HER AND SPINS HER AROUND)

ALICE: (LAUGHING THEN LOOKING HESITANTLY AT MAUDIE) I suppose it *is* a special night. Like Christmas. She allus has a glass of ginger wine at Christmas. Allright then. (SHE GOES OFF STAGE LEFT FOR ANOTHER GLASS)

CYRIL: People say there's a bloody depression on, people marchin' from bloody Jarrow, but I say there's always a bit o' brass to be med and if there was a few more smart lads like me around, Mr Baldwin wouldn't have no problems. (ALICE RETURNS AND CYRIL POURS THE THREE DRINKS) Let's drink to clever blokes like me, Alice. Let's thee and me and Alice have a drink, Maudie.

ALICE : (TAKING ONE OF THE GLASSES) Don't go chuckin' it away now tha's made it. Don't go chuckin' the money.

CYRIL: I'm too wise for that, love. Too clever by half. No, I've got just the horse that's been waiting for a little pile like this on its back. I'm wise enough to know when I'm on a lucky streak and tonight's little game proves it. Oh, I've had my eye on a certain filly for some time now. I reckon this is the time to put up.

ALICE :(IMPRESSED) I dunno – tha's a right 'un! Thee can do owt when tha sets tha mind to it. Thee can make us do owt.

CYRIL: How's it doing, Maudie? How's tha liking it? Warm thy belly, that will.

ALICE: Cyril!

CYRIL: What?

ALICE: I won't have words like that in front of Maudie. It's not decent.

CYRIL: Warm thy vitals, then, Maudie? I can say *vitals*, can I, Alice? We've all got vitals, men and women both. Vitals is the things we can't do without. Why, a motor car has got vitals, Alice. A steam engine has got vitals. All them pistons going up and down. Couldn't run without 'em. Well, Maudie, how's it going down?

MAUDIE: (COUGHS A LITTLE) It's nice.

CYRIL: Nice! Ay, that's what it is! Nice like a lot of things in life. Shouldn't wonder if tha doesn't know that. Shouldn't wonder if tha's not got a lad for instance.

MAUDIE : (EMBARRASSED) No, I've not.

ALICE: No, she's not, Cyril...

CYRIL: (POURING ANOTHER GLASS FOR ALICE) Drink up, love. It's thee deserves the treat and I'll always treat thee well when I'm in the money. (BEAT) Shouldn't wonder if she writes notes to him. Love letters to her love. (HE PUTS DOWN HIS GLASS ON THE TABLE AND RUSHES OVER TO THE SETTEE, PULLING THE EXERCISE BOOKS FROM UNDER THE CUSHIONS) Hah!

MAUDIE: (ALARMED) No, leave them alone! They're not yours!

CYRIL: Oh, I know they're not mine. I'm not educated enough to write like thee, Maudie. But I can *read*! (HE THUMBS THROUGH THEM, DROPPING SOME OF THEM ON THE FLOOR)

MAUDIE : (DESPERATELY PICKING THEM UP OFF THE FLOOR) Don't! Don't!

ALICE: (ALSO ALARMED) Don't, Cyril.

CYRIL: Don't? Don't? Why? What will you do?

MAUDIE: (ANGRY AND SCARED) I'll... I'll... I'll kill you!

CYRIL: (LAUGHS) She'll kill me? Did you hear that, Alice? Did you hear what your daughter said to me?

MAUDIE: (ALMOST HYSTERICAL NOW) I will, I will! I'll kill you!

ALICE: Maudie, you shouldn't say things like that. You shouldn't. (SHE GULPS ANOTHER DRINK) I don't know what's come over you. (TO CYRIL) Don't be angry, Cyril. Don't. It's the drink. She's not used to it. She shouldn't be having it.

CYRIL: It's not the drink, Alice. She's only had a sip, for God's sake. No, it's summat else. Summat that's in these books. Summat she doesn't want thee to know about because thee's too trusting. (GOES OVER TO TABLE, PICKS UP THE WHISKY) Have another drink, Alice. Go on. I like a woman that's got her vitals warmed. Don't be shy about it. That's more than thy daughter is. *She's* not shy.

ALICE: (FRIGHTENED NOW) What's he going on about, Maudie? What've you been up to?

CYRIL: She *has* got a lad. She writes about him. Writes *to* him, I dare say. (HE THUMBS THROUGH THE BOOK) Listen to this. Nice, this is. Real nice. For a girl of her age. Tasty. (READS WITH A SMIRK) I am the centre of the world./ I look out from inside me./ And we and you and they/ are the centres of the world/ They look out at me./ So many centres, so many worlds,/ so many people. / But only you for me, only you./ Be the centre of my world... (PAUSE) Hah! Who is he, Maudie? Who's the centre of thy world then?

MAUDIE: Nobody. Honest. It's just... it's a poem. I wrote it years ago. I did.

CYRIL: A poem? Excuse me. I may not be well educated like you, Miss School Book, but I know what a poem is. I know poems. *Forward the Light Brigade, Was there a man dismayed? Theirs not to make reply, Theirs not to reason why, Theirs but to do and die.* (BEAT) Oh, I know poems.

ALICE: Who is he, Maudie?

MAUDIE: There's no-one.

CYRIL: Years ago. Tha wrote it years ago. And kept it. Like all these others. All these poems, as tha likes to call them. Must 've been a special lad, that one. Or maybe there's more than one lad.

ALICE: Cyril, don't.

CYRIL: Only me for you, only me. Be the centre of my world. Be the centre of me, the vitals inside me, the pistons going up and down. (HE LAUGHS UPROARIOUSLY)

MAUDIE:(SHE PICKS UP GLASS FROM TABLE, JUMPS AT CYRIL, SMASHES GLASS IN HIS FACE) I'll kill you, you bastard!

ALICE: (PULLING HER OFF) Oh, you wicked girl! How could you? I won't have language like that in my house! Look what you've done to your Uncle Cyril!

43

MAUDIE : (IN TEARS) He's *not* my uncle! I hate him! (SHE FALLS BACK ON THE SETTEE)

ALICE: Cyril, Cyril, love, what's she done to thee?

CYRIL: (WIPING BLOOD FROM HIS FACE) I'm allright, woman, I'm allright. What do you think I am, some fairy that I can't stand up to a woman? Some nancy boy that I can't defend myself?

ALICE: She's not a bad girl, Cyril. But she shouldn't have done that. She shouldn't have hurt thee! And the language! I don't know where she gets it. If that's the sort of thing they teach 'em at school these days...

CYRIL: Don't go blaming schools, Alice, nor teachers neither. I bet the teachers haven't read half what's in these poems. If that's what she's still calling them. (HE IS CALMER NOW, IN CONTROL) Well, Alice, I think these poems should all be burned, that's what I think.

MAUDIE: (SHE FALLS BACK ON THE SETTEE) No! It's for school, it's...

CYRIL: Not the school work. I don't mean that. Not the spelling tests and the sums and the maps of Africa. Not the stuff she shows the teachers. I mean this love stuff that she wouldn't dare show, even to her mam. Her mam that trusts her.

MAUDIE: (ANGUISHED) No!

44

CYRIL: This stuff she keeps in cardboard boxes in her room or hides away under the cushions. That's the stuff that's got to go.

ALICE: (HUGGING HER) I'll hit her, Cyril. I'll use your belt. I'll give her a tanning. She won't forget it easily. Cutting you. Using bad language.

CYRIL: I don't want that, Alice. I'm not a hard man. I'm not a man that likes to hurt women. *You* know that.

MAUDIE: Don't burn them. Please!

ALICE: Don't, Cyril.

CYRIL: Well, seeing as this is a special day for me, my special lucky day when I've won £25 on the poker, seeing as how I had four kings on the last pot, I'm willing to be tolerant.

ALICE: Please, Cyril.

CYRIL: Although I have to say this has spoiled my night. My night which started out so well has been spoiled by all this. I don't suppose you thought about that, Maudie. I don't suppose you stopped to consider.

ALICE: She's considering now, Cyril.

CYRIL: I hope she is. I hope what tha says is right, Alice, because I know thee's a good mother. There's no doubt about it in my mind. Oh, thee's so good, Alice. But sometimes a body can be *too* good, think too well of people, trust them too much. What does tha think, Maudie? Does tha think I'm right?

MAUDIE SOBS

CYRIL: Well, does tha, Maudie?

MAUDIE: (STILL SOBBING): Yes...

CYRIL: Well, that's a beginning. That's a start. Do you love your mother, Maudie? Do you?

MAUDIE: Yes. Yes.

CYRIL: And you love these books of yours? These poems?

MAUDIE: Yes.

CYRIL: And I'm sure tha loves me, thy Uncle Cyril?

MAUDIE :(PAUSE) Yes.

CYRIL: And tha's sorry for what tha's done to me, spoiling my night?

MAUDIE: Yes.

CYRIL: Allright. Then we'll reconsider.

ALICE: Cyril, I'll get some sticking plaster. For your eye...

CYRIL: Don't worry about that, love. Get straight to bed now. I'll be with thee in no time at all. Me and Maudie are going to have a little talk. Don't worry. I'll not chastise her. Though I have the right. There's nobody here would say I didn't have the right to chastise the girl. No. Me and Maudie are friends now. I can tell. And she's sorry for what she's done.

ALICE: (RELUCTANT) Cyril, don't...

CYRIL: (IMPATIENT) What's the matter, love? Thee can go. Go.

ALICE : (FEARFUL) Cyril...

CYRIL: (IMPATIENT) Two minutes. That's all. Take the bottle up. We're not done celebrating yet. Maudie and me'll put the lights out. Isn't that right, Maudie?

MAUDIE: Yes.

ALICE: Maudie...

MAUDIE: Go, mam. Go up.

ALICE GETS UP AND LEAVES RELUCTANTLY STAGE LEFT, PICKING UP THE BOTTLE ON THE WAY. CYRIL'S EYES FOLLOW HER OUT, HE GOES OVER TO THE LIGHT SWITCH AND PUTS

IT OFF. THE STAGE IS NOW IN DARKNESS
EXCEPT FOR A SPOT OVER THE SETTEE

CYRIL: It's good that we're friends again. I won't hurt thee, Maudie. I won't hurt thy books. (HE GOES OVER TO THE SETTEE, TURNS HIS BACK ON THE AUDIENCE, TOWERS OVER MAUDIE) Quiet now. Quiet. It's only a small house and we don't want to disturb people. And I've not got much time. Because thy mother's waiting for me. She's a loving mother. I know how loving she can be. (BEAT) Thirteen, is it? Still believe in Father Christmas, do you? Well, I'm Father Christmas tonight. Here, Maudie, touch it. Touch it for luck. Ay up. It won't bite, tha knows. It's good, it's nice. Touch it proper. (SUDDENLY HIS MOOD CHANGES, HIS VOICE BECOMES ANGRY) Touch it like you'd touch a lad you was courting, all soft an' loving an' gentle like. Else you know what you'll get.

THE SPOT GOES OUT. COMPLETE DARKNESS.
MUSIC: HOLDING BACK THE YEARS BY SIMPLY
RED.

END OF ACT I

ACT II

MUSIC: SOUND OF BOMBS, AIRCRAFT. THE ALL-CLEAR. THEN MOONLIGHT SERENADE BY GLENN MILLER. THE LIGHTS GO UP ON MAUDIE AND ALICE'S HOUSE AS ALICE, MAUDIE AND DOROTHY ENTER. MAUDIE IS WEARING GLASSES AND IS CARRYING A HARDBACK COPY OF *THE RAGGED TROUSERED PHILANTHROPISTS*. THERE IS A SMALL CARPET IN PLACE OF THE PEG RUG, A RADIOGRAM IN PLACE OF THE RADIO AND THE PIANO IS NOW IN THE HOUSE. THE SETTEE HAS A DIFFERENT "THROW" ON IT AND THE TELEPHONE IS COVERED UP.)

ALICE: (SWITCHING ON THE LIGHT) Thank God for that all-clear! It's handy being right near the shelter, right near to the railway arches. But tha shouldn't go home at this hour, Dot. Tha's got to stay over.

DOROTHY: I don't know that I should...

ALICE: I said I'd invite thee. I told Maudie. I said it'll be company for Aunt Dot now Uncle Albert's out fire-watching. She'll be in need of some company, I said. I'll get us a sherry. To strengthen us nerves. I never keep strong drink in the house but I always think a sherry is cheering. Light the gas fire, Maudie. (SHE TAKES THEIR COATS OFF STAGE LEFT)

DOROTHY: What's that you were reading, Maudie?

49

MAUDIE :(STOOPING TO LIGHT THE GAS) *The Ragged Trousered Philanthropists.* It's a novel. About socialism.

DOROTHY: (UNINTERESTED): Oh, that's interesting.

ALICE : (RETURNING WITH A TRAY AND THREE GLASSES) I'm glad somebody thinks it is. Oh, tha's getting like an old woman sometimes, Maudie, the way tha's moving. Tha should get more exercise. Tha's only twenty. (TO DOROTHY) And she doesn't have to wear those glasses, not all the time.

MAUDIE: Yes I do, mam. And I'm stiff. That's why I'm moving so slow. I'm always stiff after the shelter. It's natural.

DOROTHY: Poor Maudie. You'll need some sleep if you're working tomorrow. Though it's not really tomorrow, of course, it's today.

ALICE: She'll be allright, will Maudie. She's a strong lass like her mam. Strong like her grandad. So tha *will* stay the night, Dot. Tha can have Maudie's room and she can have the settee.

DOROTHY: Is that a new one, that settee?

ALICE: We've had it a few weeks. Well, that old one was looking right miserable. You'd wonder what people got up to on that settee, the state it was in. (SHE LAUGHS)

MAUDIE: I'd like to get to bed. I've got an early start.

ALICE : (POURING THE DRINKS) Don't be rude, Maudie. Tha can't have the settee just yet because Aunt Dot is our guest and some of us want a bit of a chat and maybe a bit of a singsong.

DOROTHY : (SITTING ON THE SETTEE) Like underneath the arches.

ALICE: (SITTING ON THE CHAIR) I like it when they sing that.

DOROTHY: It's funny when you think it's true. There we are, underneath the arches, waiting for the bombs to drop. And that's what everybody's singing.

ALICE: (SINGS) Underneath the arches, waiting for the bombs to drop (ALICE AND DOROTHY COLLAPSE WITH LAUGHTER, MAUDIE IS UNMOVED)

MAUDIE: (SITTING NEXT TO DOROTHY ON SETTEE) I've got to think straight. I've some things to find, to take into work.

ALICE: Who'd've thought it - a daughter of mine workin' ont' twist drill at Balfour's? Doin' *man's* work! (SHE LAUGHS AGAIN)

MAUDIE: (ANGRILY) And only gettin' paid half what a man gets!

DOROTHY: So that's why you're reading that ragged tousled philatelists. That's why you're reading books about socialism.

ALICE: Well, what does she expect? (TO MAUDIE) Tha's only there till the men come back. Make the most of it, lass! Tha knows, Dot, we've got more money coming into this house than we ever had before, what with Maudie at Balfour's and me makin' brushes at home. I don't know what we ever needed men for, I don't. Really. Here's to the war! (SHE GIGGLES AND GULPS HER SHERRY)

DOROTHY: You talk as if you *like* the war. You talk as if you enjoy it.

MAUDIE: She likes the idea of men fighting, don't you, mam? You wish they were fighting over you.

ALICE: Keep a civil tongue in your head, Maudie. I've told thee before. (TO DOROTHY) Nay, nay, I don't say that I like the war… But I do say it's got its compensations. Oh, I know there's folk getting killed, men getting killed, good men and strong men, and more's the pity. But people are always dying, aren't they? If it's not one thing, it's another. And I do say this – people are more together when there's a war on, don't you think? More friendly. Like int' shelter tonight - all that singing. Everybody likes a bit of singing. Everybody

52

joined in. Everybody except Maudie. She'd rather read a book. I don't know where she gets all these books.

DOROTHY: Ay. All together. Joining in. I'll give you that.

MAUDIE: I joined the library, mam. That's where I get my books. It's not a mystery like where babies come from.

ALICE: I told thee to watch thy tongue. And them records as well? All that Wagner! (SHE PRONOUNCES IT WAGGONER) Opera, I ask you! You can't tell a bloody word they're singing.

MAUDIE: A friend at work. A friend at work lent me them. There's only two. (SHE SLUMPS INTO THE CHAIR)

ALICE: (TO DOROTHY) All together. Joining in. Tha's got it right, Dot. Mind you, we've always had that, Maudie and me, war or no war. I mean it's always been the two of us, looking after each other. We've never needed owt else, isn't that right, Maudie? D'you know, some people don't take us for mother and daughter, they take us for sisters. Isn't that funny? Oh, I do like this Spanish sherry. I think I'll have a fag too. I like a smoke with my drink. (SHE BEGINS TO SEARCH HER BAG, PASSING HER GLASS FROM ONE HAND TO THE OTHER) That's the only thing I don't like about them shelters – they don't let you smoke. 'Course, we can all see the reason. Still... (SHE BUMPS AGAINST THE

TABLE AND SPILLS SOME SHERRY) Oh, look what I've done, I've gone and spilt some. Eh, Maudie, get us a cloth, eh?

DOROTHY: Don't worry. I'll get it. Oh, look at Maudie. Poor lass, she's asleep. Well, that settles it, Alice. We'll just have to get to bed…

ALICE: Oh, give her a shove, that'll wake her up. I don't know, when there's us mature women bright as ninepence, talking the night away, I don't see why some young lass has got to be falling asleep all the time. This Spanish sherry came from thee and Albert, didn't it, Dot? Tell me if it's none of my business, Dot, but where do you an' Albert get this Spanish sherry? I'm right partial to a sweet sherry...

DOROTHY: But if she's working, Alice...

ALICE: It's not for hours yet. Listen, I've got a yen for a sing-song right here. Being in the shelter sort of whets my appetite. And now we've got the piano...

DOROTHY: Does it work allright? Because Albert and me couldn't never seem to get it working properly. I've always thought it needed oiling or something.

ALICE: No, it's fine. And all that sheet music too.

DOROTHY: It's all old stuff, God knows. The thing is, I've been going a bit deaf these last couple of years. Not so's anybody else would notice. But that didn't help.

(PAUSE)   Albert was very partial to them old songs once upon a time. But he changed...

ALICE: Don't they all! When you first meet 'em, they're all jumping round the dance floor, feeling your bum in the waltzes. Then when you've got them home, they sit in the chair with a glass of mild and read the racing pages.

DOROTHY: Oh, I don't know that Albert was ever a dancer...

ALICE: Oh, but he was. Like his dad. Oh, Albert were graceful. Once upon a time.

DOROTHY: Well, maybe I was never much into dancing myself. I liked the singers more than the bands. Al Bowlly. The Ink Spots.

ALICE: Oh, shame about Al Bowlly. Him getting killed. He were a very handsome man.

DOROTHY: That's what *I* thought. Actually, that's why I liked Albert. When I first met him, I though he looked a bit like Al Bowlly. Or Ivor Novello.

ALICE: Oh, I never liked Ivor Novello. A bit too...(WAVES A LIMP WRIST) for me if you know what I mean.

DOROTHY: Did you think so?

ALICE: Oh, I thought it was obvious.

DOROTHY: I never thought about it. Actually, I never do think about things like that. It's unpleasant.
(MAUDIE SLUMPS OVER ONTO DOROTHY) Ooh, your Maudie's fast.

ALICE: As long as she's not fast *and* loose. Give her a shove. Go on. No need to be gentle. Maudie's not a china cup, you know. Or if she was, she'd be the only one we've got in the house.

DOROTHY: Wake up, Maudie. Come on, you've not drunk your sherry.

MAUDIE: (WAKING SUDDENLY) What? Oh. Oh. Sorry, Aunt Dot.

ALICE: I've spilt a drop of me sherry. Get the cloth, Maudie, there's a good girl. Then we can play some songs.

MAUDIE : (GETTING UP) What about the neighbours, mam?

ALICE: Well, they're not asleep, are they? We've just had a bloody air raid. They're not going to be fast asleep. Probably do with something to cheer them up. How about Tommy Dorsey? Or Glenn Miller.

DOROTHY: I like some Glenn Miller. I like Moonlight Serenade. But I don't like them Andrews Sisters. Too tarty if you ask me.

ALICE: I know what you mean. Obvious. I hate it when a woman's obvious. Well, Maudie, is tha going for the cloth?

MAUDIE: Allright. (SHE EXITS STAGE LEFT)

DOROTHY: She's a good girl.

ALICE: I hope she is. It's the way I brought her up. Respect thyssen and others will respect thee too. That's what I tell her. That's what our dad taught Albert and me.

DOROTHY: Albert doesn't speak much of your dad.

ALICE: Does he not?

DOROTHY: But then he's not a man to reminisce about the past. Not a man for regrets, isn't Albert.

ALICE: (UNDER HER BREATH) He can't afford to be.

DOROTHY: What was that?

ALICE: I said he's always been that way. Live for today, that's Albert.

DOROTHY: I must say the piano looks nice here, as though it belongs.

ALICE: Come over more often and I'll play for the both of you. Albert can play too. I'm surprised he never did at home.

DOROTHY: Like I said, we could never seem to get it working.

ALICE: Maybe that drop of oil would've done some good. (SHE GOES OVER AND SORTS THROUGH THE SHEET MUSIC, THEN BEGINS TO PLAY AND SING) When shadows fall and trees whisper day is ending, my thoughts are ever wending home...

MAUDIE: (RETURNING) I'm sure the neighbours will want to get to sleep. They won't want to stay up all night after an air raid. (SHE WIPES UP THE SHERRY)

DOROTHY: Do you know any songs, Maudie?

ALICE: She knows Waggoner.

MAUDIE: No, I don't, Aunt Dot. Not as many as my mam knows.

DOROTHY: You must know some. Some of the new ones. Frank Sinatra and that.

MAUDIE: No. Honest. Mam, it really is late.

ALICE: (STARTS TO SING) In the wee small hours of the morning when the world around is fast asleep...

DOROTHY: Do you not go dancing then? Do you not go to the pictures.? There's lots of songs at the pictures these days. They're all musicals now. Except the war films, of course.

MAUDIE: I don't go to the pictures. Not much.

ALICE: (SINGING) Missed the Saturday dance, heard they crowded the floor, it's so different without Maudie, don't get around much any more...

DOROTHY: Don't you have a young man? You must have a young man, a lass of *your* age.

ALICE : (SINGS) All alone by the telephone, waiting for a ring a-ting a-ling...

MAUDIE: We've not got a telephone, mam.

ALICE: Wouldn't make any difference if we had. (STARTS TO SING) Underneath the arches, I dream my dreams away, underneath the arches on cobble stones I lay...

MAUDIE: I hate that. I hate it when they start singing that in the shelter. Every night. Somebody always thinks it's funny.

DOROTHY: But it's because we *are* under the arches, Maudie. Under the railway arches sheltering. That's why it's funny. Well, I think it is.

ALICE: Of course it's funny, Dot. It's a laugh. Like lots of things. It's just that Maudie doesn't have a sense of humour. Now I don't know why not. Unless it's her dad's side of the family coming out. *I've* got a sense of humour. I'm laughing all the time at this and that. And I know Albert's a laugh. He'd always had me in stitches.

DOROTHY: I think I fell in love with him because of his sense of humour.

ALICE: (UNDER HER BREATH) I think that must be why he fell for you. (THEN IN NORMAL VOICE) I thought I'd teach Maudie to play. Not complicated stuff. Not Waggoner. But ordinary, nice songs that we could all enjoy. That was one of the reasons I was glad to get our dad's piano back. It was very good of thee to let us have it, Dot. But Maudie doesn't have any musical talent.

DOROTHY: But you're good with words, aren't you, Maudie? Albert's always saying you're good with words.

ALICE: Well, if she is, she hides the bloody fact. Pardon my language. She doesn't have a word to say half the time.

DOROTHY: I mean writing words *down*. Compositions. Poems. I heard she was always good at poems at school.

ALICE: (SUDDENLY ANGRY) Well, she's not at school now.

MAUDIE: I'm at work, mam. That's what pays for the carpet and the radiogram.

ALICE: Oh, we owe it all to you, do we?

MAUDIE: Some of it.

ALICE: And my brushes. I make them brushes. Don't forget them.

MAUDIE: Allright.

ALICE: (TO DOROTHY) You'd think we was at each other's throats all the time if you didn't know us. But we're not. We look after each other. We do have a row now and again but that's because we're so close. We practically know what each other's thinking. It's like I said, I don't know why we bother with men, I really don't. Not when we've got each other.

MAUDIE: It's like me and the job at Balfour's.

DOROTHY: How d'you mean?

MAUDIE: When the men come back, it'll all change.

ALICE : (SLAMS DOWN LID OF PIANO) What does tha mean by that, my girl? Just what does tha mean by that?

MAUDIE: Oh, nothing. Nothing. I'm tired.

DOROTHY: We're *all* tired.

ALICE: No, we're not. Normal people aren't tired. Not all the time. Normal people aren't tired of life. And *I'm* normal people.

MAUDIE: And *I'm* not?

ALICE: Not the way tha carries on.

MAUDIE: And how do I carry on?

ALICE: Like... like... like tha's got no respect for me, or for thyssen. Like tha's got no time for life, for having any fun.

MAUDIE: You mean men again. You mean like having any men.

ALICE: Maudie!

DOROTHY: Oh, she didn't mean it that way, I'm sure.

MAUDIE: Yes, she did. She can't understand why any daughter of hers doesn't have loads of men, the way *she's* had loads of men.

DOROTHY: No, I meant that *you* didn't mean it. I know *she* meant it.

ALICE: Don't think tha's getting away with being rude to me, my girl. God pays his debts and so do I. You're not too big, you know, not too big for me to...

MAUDIE: To do what? Take off your belt to me? Is it chastisement, then? Is that what I deserve? To be chastised?

ALICE: I don't know what tha's on about. (TO DOROTHY) It's the drink talking.

DOROTHY: But she's only had one sherry.

ALICE: She's not used to it.

DOROTHY: (PEACEMAKING) Well, we're tired. It's been a lively night with bombers an' all. We should really get some sleep now. (TO ALICE) She doesn't mean anything.

ALICE: Allright, Dot, let's you and me get up them stairs. We'll take some of this Spanish sherry with us eh? No point leaving it to go to waste with madam here.

THEY EXIT STAGE LEFT

MAUDIE : (TO AUDIENCE) *Sherry*. Six letters. A fortified wine from Spain. (BEAT) *Port*. Four letters. A fortified wine from Portugal. Starboard side, port side. Port Said in Egypt. Porthole. Portmanteau. Porterhouse steak. Oh, Mr Porter, what shall I do? Any port in a

storm. (SHE SINKS DOWN ON THE SETTEE. THE
LIGHTS GO DOWN.)

MUSIC: WHAT'LL I DO? BY DICK HAYMES.
ENTER STAGE RIGHT ALICE IN HAT AND
OVERCOAT AND HARRY IN US MILITARY
UNIFORM. PICKED OUT BY THE SPOTLIGHT,
THEY WALK, HAND IN HAND, TO CENTRE
FRONT OF STAGE. THEY KISS LINGERINGLY.
FINALLY THEY SEPARATE, BREATHLESS.)

ALICE: Do they all kiss as good as you where you come
from?

HARRY: Nope. Nobody does it like me. Nobody does it
like you either.

ALICE: (GIGGLES) Oh, I wouldn't say that.

HARRY: Believe me, I know. I've kissed a lot of ladies
in my time.

ALICE: And I bet you do more than kissing when you
get the chance.

HARRY: (LAUGHS) A gentleman never talks about it.

ALICE: Most men I know never talk about it because
they never do it.

HARRY: How d'you know they never do it?

ALICE: You only have to look at them. Who'd they get to do it with? Who'd put up with 'em? Oh, I'm sick of the men round here, I really am. You Yanks are a breath of fresh air.

HARRY: Not everybody seems to think so.

ALICE: They're just jealous. Like I said. They're not real men, they're soft. All the men that's left. All the men that didn't join up. Took the soft option. Job down the pit. Munitions work.

HARRY: My dad was a coalminer. Pennsylvania is big coalmining country. It's a tough job.

ALICE: Oooh, Pennsylvania! (SINGS) Da-dee-dah, Call Pennsylvania Six-five-thousand. (BACK TO SPEAKING) I bet it's nice there. I bet it's nothing like this.

HARRY: Well, sure it's nice. But you've got some nice places over here.

ALICE: Yeah. (LOOKING ROUND) And this isn't one of them. Tell me about Pennsylvania. I don't mean about the coalmining, either. I know about coalmining. What are the people like?

HARRY: They're just people. People are the same all over.

ALICE: No, they're not. Not like the people round here. *You're* not like the people round here, Harry.

HARRY: Why? Because of my accent?

ALICE: Because you smile and you laugh and you're full of sunshine.

HARRY: No. Sunshine's *California*. Pennsylvania's not sunshine. Anyway, most people don't think I'm full of sunshine. Most people think I'm full of something else. Something I shouldn't mention in front of a lady.

ALICE: I bet they don't. I bet they say you're big and strong and full of sunshine, like I said. Anyway, if the sun only shines in California, you could always move there. At least you don't have to cross the bloody Atlantic to do it.

HARRY: You said bloody!

ALICE: (TAKEN ABACK) What?

HARRY: They tell us not say it. Not with English people. They say it's a swear word over here. Isn't that right?

ALICE: First time *I've* heard of it. You don't hear bad language from *me*.

HARRY: So they got it wrong?

ALICE: Language is a funny thing. When you're a foreigner.

HARRY: They tell you such dumb things, these top brass. They don't know a damn thing really. Sorry, I mean darn thing.

ALICE: Apology accepted. Still, I suppose I'd have a few language problems if I lived in America. You'd have to teach me.

HARRY: Is that where you'd like to be right now?

ALICE: Oh yeah. I could just see myself. I could. I suit a suntan, me. I'm not one of your pale-skinned English roses that go all red when they've been out on a charabanc trip to Blackpool. Oh no. Me and the sun get on. It's just that we don't see that much of each other so we don't get to form what you might call a lasting friendship. But I could stand to see some more of him. I could stand to see some of America.

HARRY: Just for a visit? Or for settling down?

ALICE: If you're going to do a thing, you might as well do it right. Go the whole hog. I wouldn't mind living in the US of A. I wouldn't mind meeting film stars in California and seeing a lot more sun. Why stay here? What's it got that's so great?

HARRY: But it's your home. And when the war's over, things'll get better. Everybody is a little sentimental about their home. Their family.

ALICE: Not me. I've always been a bit of a rover, deep down. I've just never had a chance to do it.

HARRY: But you have a daughter?

ALICE: Maudie.

HARRY: What about Maudie? Is she like you?

ALICE: No, *she's* not a rover.

HARRY: You'd have to take her too.

ALICE: If I went to America?

HARRY: If you went anywhere.

ALICE: To be honest with you, she wouldn't want to come. She's too close to her uncle and her Aunt Dot. No, I don't think we'd have to worry about Maudie... (STRIVING TO GET AWAY FROM THE SUBJECT) Your dad was a coalminer, was he? I'm sure you're right about coal miners. Some of them anyway. I'm sure your dad was a real man like his son. But half of them as go downt'pit round here end up sweeping the offices because they're not even good enough for t'coalface. There's all sorts call theirselves miners now. Bevin Boys. *Boys* is right. Not men. (SHE STROKES THE

68

LAPEL OF HIS UNIFORM) It takes real men to do the fighting, real men to protect us families. (THEY KISS AGAIN BEFORE BREAKING APART)

ALICE: You can come in, you know. It's OK. Better than out here with neighbours nosing through their curtains. See. (SHE POINTS OFFSTAGE) You can see. There. Them chinks of light over by the off-licence. It's dangerous, that is. Some of 'em would rather be bombed out than miss anything juicy. It's got so a respectable woman can't even take advantage of the blackout.

HARRY: Is that what you are, Alice? A respectable woman?

ALICE : (COY) I told you I was. Well, until I met you, I was. You have to be when you've got a young daughter. Children are very impressionable. My husband's been dead a few years now, like I told you. And I've kept myself decent because a mother has responsibilities. But you... well, you've managed to get round me. I think it's because you're a Yank, because you're different. You've got different ways and they get round me because I'm not used to them. Are you coming in? Maudie's on nights this week.

HARRY: On nights? I didn't think she was old enough to work.

ALICE: (QUICKLY) Well, she isn't. Not really. She helps her uncle. My brother. Like I said, they're very close. Just a couple of evenings in the office. And then she stays over at his house. We just *call* it working nights. It's a family joke. It all helps her with her school work.

HARRY: I'd like to meet her.

ALICE: Well, she's very shy. Young girls are. I was shy when I was her age. I'm still quite shy now.

HARRY: Does she look like her mother?

ALICE: Oh no, she never inherited my looks. She's got brains though. She's good with words. So she tells me.

HARRY: She sounds interesting.

ALICE: She is. Not pretty, but interesting. And tonight she's out of the way, Loo-tenant Morgenstern. We've got the house to usselves. Come on. You're a very lucky man. It's not often I make an offer like this. (STARTS PULLING HIM BY THE HAND)

HARRY: (LAUGHING) OK, respectable lady. But I got to warn you - I got to get up early tomorrow. I have things to do.

ALICE: Important things, is it? Secret missions?

HARRY: Hardly. Secrecy isn't my line. Getting it in the papers is my line.

ALICE: (HESITATES) Getting it in the papers? How d'you mean?

HARRY: Well, not *your* papers, not the ones over here. It's the papers back home, and not just the big cities: I do my bit for the small towns as well.

ALICE: What do you do with newspapers?

HARRY: Send them stories. About our boys. You know, I talk to them while they're over here, while they're still on friendly soil, get a few quotes for the people back home, get some pictures taken, send the copy over. It's a big thing for the folks back in the States. And for the kids as well.

ALICE: And what do you call it, this job?

HARRY: It's called public relations liaison.

ALICE: Public relations! But you're an officer in a uniform…

HARRY: Sure. I'm military personnel. But I guess it's kind of honorary.

ALICE : (ANGRILY PULLING HER HAND AWAY) You're a Bevin Boy!

HARRY : (CONFUSED) What?

ALICE: Oh, I don't mean you're *really* a Bevin Boy. I
don't mean you go downt' pit. I don't think they'd take
you. But that's what you are. The same sort of thing.
You're a bloke that's stayed out of the fighting.

HARRY : (ALSO GETTING ANGRY) Hold on, hold
on! Let me tell you – my stories are important. For the
kids that go into battle. For their folks back home. My
stories help the war effort.

ALICE: Telling stories. Words. That's always a man's
thing is words. Words to get out of things. Words to get
out of the war. Good with words. Oh, I know who'd get
on with you!

HARRY: Now wait a minute!

ALICE: (SHE STOPS HERSELF) This wife of yours…

HARRY: (AWKWARDLY) We talked about that
already.

ALICE: You're really going to divorce her, Harry? Tha
wasn't lying to me about that?

HARRY: We were already planning it. The war just
made things easier.

ALICE: Easier for some. And why should I believe
you?

HARRY: I never lied to you, Alice…

ALICE : Course not. It must be one of them language problems. Like not knowing when to say *bloody*. All full of sunshine. Well, I'll give you some sunshine! (SHE TAKES HIS HAND AGAIN AND PULLS HIM TOWARDS STAGE LEFT) There's still a few things I'm good at. And I don't want her over the off-licence seeing how good I am. (HE GRINS AS THEY EXIT STAGE LEFT)

LIGHTS GO OUT. MUSIC: SOMEONE TO WATCH OVER ME BY FRANK SINATRA. WHEN THE MUSIC FADES AND THE LIGHTS GO UP, MAUDIE IS SITTING AT THE TABLE WITH ALICE WHO IS IN AN APRON. ALICE LUNGES ACROSS TABLE AND GRABS MAUDIE BY THE WRIST

ALICE: (SHOUTING) Don't tell me it's none of my business! Don't talk to your mother like that! Tha's not too old to get a good hiding off me, my girl! The way I should've done when tha was little, the way thy grandad would've done! Oh, I blame the place tha's working in - it's given thee ideas above thyssen. Though I can't see it lastin' much longer - there's plenty of lads comin' home lookin' for work an' tha's best make up tha mind to find thyssen a decent chap as'll treat thee proper.

MAUDIE: But I've *got* a chap, mam. And he *is* decent and proper!

ALICE: Decent and proper and *married*! Which means he's only decent an' proper with woman he's married to!

73

MAUDIE: He's getting a divorce.

ALICE: Divorce! Is he then? How long's he been tellin'
thee that? Three years, is it? Three years tha's been
carryin' on an' I never knew about it! I wouldn't know
today if it weren't for that Dorothy! Though I should've
guessed. Them books! Them bloody records! Pagliacci!
(SHE SOUNDS THE G) Oh, that woman's been waitin'
for summat like this an' now it's come! You should've
seen 'er! Smile like a Cheshire cat! That's what hurts as
much as owt - her bein' the one that telled me!

MAUDIE: She had no right.

ALICE: She had every right. She's your auntie.

MAUDIE : Well, it makes no difference.

ALICE: It makes a difference to *me*, lass!

MAUDIE: I don't see why it should. You an' your men!
How many is it, mam, or have you never tallied up?

ALICE SLAPS MAUDIE HARD. THEN SHE BURSTS
INTO TEARS AND HUGS THE SOBBING GIRL

ALICE: Oh Maudie, just look at thyssen. Tha's twenty-
seven years old and tha knows nowt. Tha knows nowt
about *men* at any rate, or he wouldn't have got thee in
this scrape. Men? I've had men allright, but not one as I
knew were married, not one as I knew were married

when I met 'im. What's he do, this Barry? Senior draughtsman, is it? What's that when it's at 'ome? It's not a *man's* job. I'll senior draughtsman 'im! Does his wife know?

MAUDIE : (IN BETWEEN SOBS) Course she does. Course she knows.

ALICE: *I* bet!

MAUDIE: She knows, I tell you. They don't get on, haven't got on for years, long before him an' me...

ALICE: Happen she never liked Waggoner. (BEAT) What about bairns? Have they got bairns?

MAUDIE: (BREAKING OUT OF THE EMBRACE, RUNNING ACROSS TO THE SETTEE): There's only Anthony. He's seven. Barry and his wife, they've not had... relations. Not for years.

ALICE: Happen he's been doin' allright for hissen all the same.

MAUDIE: It's the child we're waiting on. Till he's older and can understand...

ALICE: Well, *I* understand, my girl, and I'll tell thee what we're going to do. I'll get me coat an' we'll go round and have a little talk with *Missus* Senior Draughtsman and find out what she really knows and what she's got to say for hersen.

MAUDIE: Mam!

ALICE: Come on, luv. Come on, Maudie. I'm goin' by myssen if I 'ave to, but it's best if tha see for thyssen which way the wind blows. It's all fort' best, I promise. Oh, come on, Maudie. (SHE WALKS ACROSS STAGE RIGHT, PICKS UP HER COAT, STANDS WAITING) Come on, girl!

SHE GRABS MAUDIE AND THEY STRUGGLE AND FALL ON THE FLOOR, FINALLY MAUDIE IS REDUCED TO SUBMISSION. ALICE SITS ASTRIDE HER

ALICE: You know it's for the best, Maudie. You know it is really. You know it wouldn't work with a married man. It's dishonest and I hate dishonesty. (SHE CARESSES MAUDIE THEN GETS TO HER FEET AND TAKES OFF HER APRON) You know I'm right, Maudie. You know when I'm right. You know you do.

EXIT ALICE, TAKING HER COAT, STAGE LEFT. MAUDIE TAKES OFF HER SHOES AND SINKS BACK ON THE SETTEE. SHE TAKES THE "MODERN" SETTEE COVER AND PLACES IT OVER THE SETTEE. THE PHONE RINGS AND MAUDIE UNCOVERS THE PHONE AND PICKS UP THE RECEIVER

MAUDIE: (INTO TELEPHONE) Yes, Dot. I was visiting this afternoon. I had another word with the sister.

SHE PUTS PHONE DOWN, LIGHT DIMS ON SETTEE, MAUDIE WALKS ACROSS TO SISTER'S DESK AS SPOTLIGHT FALLS ON IT

SISTER: You've made the arrangements then?

MAUDIE: As much as I can. It won't be a problem.

SISTER: And you've found out about the allowance? You've filled in the forms?

MAUDIE: I've filled in the forms.

SISTER: How is your mother today? I mean I've been to see her of course. But I wondered how *you* found her, how she was with you.

MAUDIE: She said she didn't understand why she was in here. She said you could understand with some of 'em. *Two bricks short of a load, some of 'em are.* That's what she said. She's very forthright, my mother. *And they smell, Maudie, she said, they smell! I'll start smelling like that if I have to stay here, I know I will.*

SISTER: We don't let our patients smell. We keep our patients clean.

MAUDIE: Maybe when you work here, you don't notice it. But I don't want her smelling. I told her she'd be allright. I said it wouldn't be for long. I said: *They wouldn't keep you in if they didn't need to, would they? And she said: Wouldn't they? Oh wouldn't they? There's nowt wrong wi' me, lass. You know that, Maudie. Nowt wrong that bein' home wouldn't cure!* (BEAT) She's a suspicious woman is my mother. Difficult at the best of times.

SISTER: It's to be hoped you can look after her then.

MAUDIE: That's what we do, Mam and me. We look after each other. (SHE RETURNS TO THE PHONE AS LIGHT GOES OUT OVER SISTER'S DESK AND COMES ON OVER SETTEE, SHE SPEAKS INTO PHONE) Hello again, Dot. No, you can visit any time. Mam would be glad to see you. Yes, she'd know you. She'd know who you are. I'm sure she would. Probably. I know you've had trouble with your legs. I understand. Saturday. She'll probably come home Saturday. I'll cope. No, I haven't thought it all out. But it's home. It's her home. Where shadows fall and trees whisper day is ending. Underneath the arches on cobblestones so grey. I know you'll come over and help. When you can. I know about your leg trouble. I'll cope. I'll work something out. Don't worry, Aunt Dot. Yes, it's a shame there's not a man about. But mam and me look after each other. We don't need a man. (PUTS DOWN PHONE, TURNS TO AUDIENCE) We don't need a man now, we're too old to know what to do with him. (SHE PULLS BACK LATEST COVER ON SETTEE, COVERS PHONE)

78

Well, I'm tired. I need my rest. (SHE LIES DOWN AS LIGHTS DIM)

MUSIC: ARE YOU LONESOME TONIGHT? BY ELVIS PRESLEY. WHEN MUSIC FADES AND LIGHTS GO UP, MAUDIE IS STANDING IN THE LIVING ROOM, STAGE RIGHT, WEARING A COAT. ALICE, NOW GREY-HAIRED, IS STANDING BY THE TABLE, WHICH HAS A DIFFERENT TABLECLOTH, ARTHUR IS SITTING ON THE SETTEE WHICH HAS ITS SIXTIES THROW AND THERE ARE TWO CHAIRS THAT MATCH AND A NEW CARPET. THERE IS ALSO A DANSETTE RECORD PLAYER AND A SMALL-SCREEN TV SET IN PLACE OF THE RADIOGRAM AND PIANO.

MAUDIE: You know we'll be late if we don't hurry, mam. You know we will.

ALICE: (SHE IS SORTING THROUGH BATCHES OF OLD PHOTOS ON THE TABLE. THE PHOTOS ARE HELD TOGETHER BY RUBBER BANDS AND STORED IN A SHOE BOX) I didn't think it started at half past seven. Oh, look at this one, Maudie (REFERRING TO ONE OF THE PHOTOS) That was when your Uncle Albert took us to Whitby. Do you remember? Oh, we did have a good time! (BEAT) I thought it were eight o'clock. I swear it said eight o'clock int' *Star*, Maudie, I'm sure it did.

MAUDIE: No. I told you exactly when it was starting. I told you both. Now we're late for the bus. It's separate performances and you can't get in after it's started. It's a rule.

ARTHUR: I never heard that one before.

MAUDIE: It's Alfred Hitchcock's own rule.

ARTHUR: Well, I don't mind. I were only goin' for thy sake, Alice. I don't get to the pictures much. Well, you can see it all on telly these days. (HE GETS UP, GOES ACROSS TO IMAGINARY MIRROR, BRUSHES HIS THIN WHITE HAIR WITH HIS HAND)

ALICE: Don't say that. Not after all the trouble Maudie went to, missing her evening class. You'd enjoy it, I expect. It's a good film.

ARTHUR: How d'you know? (HE WAGS A FINGER AT HER) How d'you know it's a good film if you've not seen it? Tell us, go on. Eh, I've got you there, girl.

ALICE: Because everybody says it's good. (SHE STARTS PUTTING THE PHOTOS BACK INTO THE BOX) It's Alfred Hitchcock. Everybody knows he's good, Alfred Hitchcock. And it's got that actor in it, him that's very thin.

MAUDIE: Anthony Perkins. (BEAT) Well, I suppose we're not going, are we? You light the gas fire, mam, The kettle's boiled so I might as well pour some coffee. (SHE GOES OUT TO THE KITCHEN, STAGE LEFT)

ALICE: (MAINLY TO HERSELF) I like the pictures, always have done. I mean *going* to the pictures. But I like these kind of pictures better. (INDICATING PHOTOS) When I was a kid, it wasn't usual for people to have cameras, but *we* had one. And I saved them all, all the photos. But nowadays... D'you know, we've still got that bloody box camera. I keep going on at Maudie to get something up-to-date, but she takes no interest. It's not that we can't afford it. (COMING OUT OF HER REVERIE) I never knew they wouldn't let you in once the picture started though. I've never heard that one before. Have you, Arthur? I've never heard o' that.

ARTHUR: I don't go much, love. (HE SETTLES BACK ON THE SETTEE AND UNBUCKLES HIS BELT) There, that's better.

ALICE : (GOING ACROSS TO HIM, HUGGING HIM): Tha's putting on weight. Tha'll have to go on a diet.

ARTHUR : (CUDDLING HER) Nay, I'm just well built. Tha doesn't want to nag me. Now, what's this night school Maudie's goin' to?

ALICE: She's learning shorthand. So she can be a secretary. Well, they all need shorthand these days. And she's wasted with what she's doing now. Just filing things and writing in ledgers. Not that it'll do her much good when she's got qualified because she's too old, because there's all them young girls she'll have to work with. And they'll be the ones that get promotion. But she's wasted. She's got brains, allright. I've always said that. But she's never used 'em. She should've stayed on at school. She was good at school. Good with words. So typing ought to suit her down to the ground. You need qualifications these days for everything. And she's no spring chicken any more.

ARTHUR: She should've wed. I don't hold with women working.

ALICE: Don't let Maudie catch you saying that. Bit late in the day for that! But you're right, duck, she's wasted herself with men as well. Not like her mam.

SHE SQUEEZES HIS HAND. HE GIVES AN EXCITED LAUGH. MAUDIE RETURNS WITH TRAY OF COFFEE

ALICE: Here. Give us one, duck. Ooh 'eck...! (AS SHE TAKES THE CUP, SHE SPILLS SOME COFFEE) Oh, look at that! (SHE PUTS DOWN THE CUP, TAKES A HANKIE OUT OF HER HANDBAG AND STARTS MOPPING UP) This carpet shows every stain. We could do with a new one, one o' them carpets like Dot's got, wall to wall. She won't like that. She doesn't like other people havin' same as she's got. Oh, get us a cloth, there's a good girl. We can afford a new carpet, can't we?

MAUDIE: I suppose. Here, *I'll* do it, mam. I'll get a cloth. Tell Arthur his coffee's there. Don't let him knock it over too.

ALICE: (CONTINUING TO MOP UP) What do you think about the carpet, Arthur? We've been in this house, Maudie an' me, since she were a kid, you know, but it's *your* house now as much as it's... (SHE LOOKS UP) Well, look at that. Just look at that. He's asleep. Just like that. Fast asleep. Dead to the world.

MAUDIE: He's tired, mam, he's old.

ALICE: (OUTRAGED) Old? He's not *old*. He's *my* age. I won't 'ave 'im old! (SHE JABS HER ELBOW INTO ARTHUR'S SIDE) Wake up, you silly bugger!

ARTHUR: (WAKING WITH A START) What? What? Are we goin' then? Are we goin' after all?

ALICE: (RESIGNED) Nay. If we went, tha'd likely fall asleep an' we might not be able to wake thee an' tha's such a fat lump, we'd have to ask somebody to carry thee home. (TO MAUDIE) He's *not* old.

MAUDIE: Allright, he's not old.

ALICE: And *I'm* not old.

MAUDIE: You're 62. I'm turned 40 meself. You're good for your age, mam. Well preserved.

ALICE: Well preserved! You've got an unkind tongue sometimes, Maudie.

MAUDIE: Don't shout, mam. You'll wake him up again.

ALICE: Oh, but he's useless. If we're not going out, then I can look at my photos again. They *are* good, aren't they? (SHE GOES BACK TO THE TABLE)

MAUDIE: They're very good, mam.

ALICE: It was good of Dot to give 'em to us. But I suppose she's no use for them now Albert's passed on. I mean, there's no pictures of *her* family. I don't think I've ever seen any. Maybe they never took a good picture. *She* never did. But look at these. Look at your Uncle Albert. And me. And your grandad. He was a nipper when they built that Woodhead Tunnel, Maudie, fetching and carrying for the excavators. His dad died of the cholera with 30 others that was buildin' it and your grandad was the man of the family then! Oh, such a man 'e was! Oh, it's a shame you never knew him! It's a shame!

MAUDIE: I know, mam, I've heard it all.

ALICE: Well, it's right you should hear these things. It's right you should know. There was never another like him and there never will be.

MAUDIE: I'm sure you're right. (MAUDIE GOES OVER AND SITS AT TABLE WITH ALICE)

ALICE: I *am* right and no mistake about it. Oh, Albert had his fine points. I'm not saying owt bad about Albert.

But he couldn't measure up. I don't know what Dot saw in him in that way, I don't.

MAUDIE: Mam, he was your brother. That's not a nice thing to say.

ALICE: Well, he can't hear me, can he? And if he can, he'll understand. And your dad...

MAUDIE: I don't remember my dad.

ALICE: He had no idea. He was always... I don't know. Flowers and things. Words. I've never been good with words. I never liked words. It's supposed to be a woman's thing is words, but I was never struck. And then there was... what was his name?

MAUDIE: Oh mam, we're not having Memory Lane, are we? I don't think I can stand it.

MAUDIE GOES TO SIT IN CHAIR ON OPPOSITE SIDE OF ROOM

ALICE: He was always doing jobs, tidying up, doing the housework...

MAUDIE: Tom. I liked Tom. I liked Dad, I think. Oh, I don't remember!

ALICE: And then Cyril...

MAUDIE: (QUICKLY) I remember *Cyril*. (PAUSE) Don't go on, mam. I can't remember all their names. *You* can't remember.

ALICE: And this one...

MAUDIE: And you better not let Arthur hear you comparing him with all your other men. How do you think he'll feel? He thinks you were dead respectable before you met him. He even thinks you married my dad.

ALICE: Well, I would have done. If he'd been anything like.

MAUDIE: I suppose he must've been like me, my dad. That's why *we're* not like each other, you and me.

ALICE: I suppose he must. Oh, I've made some mistakes in my life, Maudie, but I've always been proud of one thing. I've always been proud of thee. It's always been thee and me, sticking together. I've always looked after thee.

MAUDIE: Always.

ALICE: I know we've had our differences. Over that Barry...

MAUDIE: Don't, mam!

ALICE: But I've always done my best. Whatever I've done, it's been for thy good.

MAUDIE: It's too late to go to my class tonight. I'll have a go at the crossword.

ALICE: We could watch telly. It's *Z Cars*.

MAUDIE: I'll do the crossword.

ALICE: Arthur likes *Z Cars*. I'd better wake him.

MAUDIE: I wouldn't bother, mam. He won't thank you for it.

ALICE: But I don't want him to sleep. You know what he's like once he drops off. That's it for the night. He's no good to me then.

MAUDIE: Well, he *has* dropped off. Give him a rest, mam. Just this once.

ALICE: It's not right him sleeping all the time. And he *does* like *Z Cars*. You know he does, Maudie.

MAUDIE: I wouldn't wake him, mam. Honest.

ALICE: I'd like to see him… I'd like to see him... awake. It'd make a change.

ALICE GOES OVER TO HIM AND PUSHES HIM

ALICE: Come on, Arthur. Come on. It's *Z Cars*. You know you like it. Come on.

MAUDIE: (LOOKING HARD AT ARTHUR) Mam...

ALICE: Come on, Arthur...

MAUDIE: Mam...

MAUDIE GETS TO HER FEET AND MOVES
NERVOUSLY ACROSS TO ALICE. ARTHUR
SUDDENLY FALLS OVER ON HIS SIDE

ALICE: Oh! Oh! Maudie! What...!

MAUDIE: (GRABBING HOLD OF ARTHUR,
PROPPING HIM UP, UNBUTTONING HIS SHIRT)
Phone for an ambulance!

ALICE: He's not breathing! He's stopped breathing!

MAUDIE: Phone for an ambulance! You talk, mam.
You tell them. Ambulance. Give them the address. (SHE
PICKS ARTHUR UP AND LAYS HIM ON THE
FLOOR, SHE PUMMELS HIS CHEST AND
ATTEMPTS TO GIVE HIM THE KISS OF LIFE AS
ALICE DIALS 999)

ALICE : (INTO PHONE): Ambulance! Ambulance! It's
Arthur! Arthur Crosby!

MAUDIE: The address! Give them the address!

ALICE: He's stopped breathing!

MAUDIE: Give them the address!

ALICE: He's stopped breathing!

MAUDIE: (SCREECHING) Give them the bloody address!

LIGHTS OFF. MUSIC: THE FUNERAL MARCH. AS IT FADES, ALICE AND MAUDIE AND DOROTHY ENTER AT BACK STAGE RIGHT AND ALICE SITS AT THE TABLE WITH THE OTHER TWO STANDING AROUND HER. THEY ALL WEAR BLACK COATS AND HATS

ALICE: One of the best. That was what it said on the banner on the coffin. All those men from Forgemasters. I never knew he had so many friends.

MAUDIE: Don't cry, mam. You've still got *me*.

ALICE: One of the best indeed! Well, if he were one o' the best, I never found out what 'e were best at. If he were one o' the best, I'd hate to meet one o' the worst, that's all I can say.

MAUDIE: Hush, mam.

ALICE: I will not.

MAUDIE: Tell her to hush, Aunt Dot.

DOROTHY: Maudie's right. Leave him alone, poor devil. He's gone to meet his Maker now.

ALICE: It's not his Maker he's ever had to bother with. It's me he should've bothered about. More than he did. A lot more!

DOROTHY: Don't make a scene. You were very good at our *Albert's* funeral. You know you were.

ALICE: Albert was allright wi' us. Left us the house, didn't he? Oh, Albert was a good man like his dad. But this one - he'd not been a man since... since I can't remember. I can't. Tell 'er, Maudie. Tell 'er I'm speaking the truth.

MAUDIE: Please, mam...

ALICE: I'm well rid, I don't mind telling you. Just Maudie an' me now, like it always was. And it's a good job that lot didn't come back for ham sandwiches. We've nowt int' fridge anyway. And I don't know the half of 'em. I wouldn't mind if they was kin, but he had no blood relatives except for a second cousin in Clitheroe. And *she's* not come!

MAUDIE: It'll be just us, you and me and Aunt Dorothy. We'll sit down with a piece of cake and a glass of sherry and remember him. He wasn't that bad, mam.

ALICE: I'm not very keen on sherry, luv. Have we not got some Johnnie Walker left over from Christmas? I suppose I'll miss 'im though. You do miss people, don't you? Funny how you do. You'd miss me, wouldn't you, Maudie?

LIGHTS OFF. MUSIC: PRETTY VACANT BY THE SEX PISTOLS. AS MUSIC FADES, LIGHTS GO UP ON THE HOUSE: THE RECORD PLAYER AND SMALL TV HAVE BEEN REPLACED BY CD PLAYER, COLOUR TV AND VIDEO. MAUDIE AND ALICE FACE EACH OTHER ACROSS THE SETTEE, WHICH HAS A NEW "THROW." THEY ARE DRESSED IN THEIR INDOOR CLOTHES

MAUDIE: I've been missing it three days. And the money's been drawn.

ALICE: I know nowt. What're you saying? I've got to run. I want to go to the lavatory.

MAUDIE: My pension book. You took it. You took it and you cashed it.

ALICE: (DESPERATELY) I was goin' to tell you. I thought: Save 'er the trouble, I'll do it for 'er when I get my own. That's what I thought.

MAUDIE: But you never did tell me.

ALICE: I forgot.

MAUDIE: Where's the money then?

ALICE: I forget. I mean, I get confused. It's in me purse. *One* of me purses. I don't remember which.

MAUDIE: You took it out of my dresser. Other things too. I'm not angry, mam, but I've got to know.

ALICE: No. You must've left it lying about. I did it to save you trouble, that's all. What other things?

MAUDIE: Private things. Old things. Papers.

ALICE: Papers? (SUDDENLY ANGRY) Letters, you mean. Letters from that Barry. Letters from that fancy man of yours! That married man! I thought I'd put a stop to that!

MAUDIE: *Old* letters.

ALICE: *Dirty* letters. I read them, didn't I?. Dirty. That's the only word to describe them. We shouldn't 'ave letters like that in our house. You shouldn't keep such letters.

MAUDIE: What've you done with my letters?

ALICE: Burned 'em. Threw 'em away. I don't know. I forget. (MAUDIE HOLDS UP A PILE OF EXERCISE BOOKS, PAPERS AND PHOTOS HELD TOGETHER BY ELASTIC BANDS) My drawers! Those are out of my drawers! You don't go in my drawers, madam!

MAUDIE: The letters belong to me. You took them.

ALICE: I never. He still writes, doesn't he? Your fancy man. You think I don't know but I do.

MAUDIE: No, he doesn't, mam, not since... They're old, mam, honest. He's never written since... You know. You remember.

ALICE: You blame me. You blame me for stopping it, for seeing his wife about it. But it weren't right. It weren't. I had to. It were dishonest.

MAUDIE: I don't blame you, mam. Really.

ALICE: I don't know why you're making all this fuss if you don't blame me. What's all the fuss about? And those photos! (POINTS AT BUNDLE IN MAUDIE'S HAND) Don't touch those photos, those are mine! Put them back! I didn't take your letters.

MAUDIE: They were in your drawer, mam. Your photos and *my* letters.

ALICE: You've no rights looking there.

MAUDIE: You've no rights taking my things. My letters. I just kept them, just to remember.

ALICE : (HER ATTENTION WANDERING) Kept them to remember. Photos of me dad, your uncle Albert, people, people I like to remember, men... (ANGRY AGAIN) And I've seen in there! (SHE SNATCHES

ONE OF THE EXERCISE BOOKS) I've seen what you've written. You ought to be ashamed, you ought. And you're the one supposed to have brains, supposed to be educated! You're the one supposed to write poetry! Call this poetry? (SHE OPENS THE BOOK AND READS) The last time I saw Paris, her heart was young and gay. You are my sunshine, my only sunshine. I don't want to set the world on fire. That old black magic's got me in its spell... oh, pages an' pages of it! The bloody book's full of it! Call that poetry?

MAUDIE: I don't call it poetry, mam. They're names of songs, that's all. (SHE WIPES HER EYES)

ALICE: Names of songs? Course they're names of songs. Think I don't know that? I know all the songs, I do! I suppose they're the names of the songs you an' your fancy man liked!

MAUDIE: Barry *did* like songs. Ordinary songs. Not just opera. Not all the time. But I was never good at remembering songs. Never good at remembering the words.

ALICE: Poetry! You couldn't write poetry! You never could! Pages an' pages of names of songs! That's all you were good for writing! That's all!

MAUDIE: I'm taking my things, mam. I'm going to my room.

ALICE: (BREAKING DOWN) Oh Maudie, I'm sorry. I didn't mean to read 'em. I must've picked them up, tidied them away, picked them up by mistake where you'd dropped them. That must be it. Eh, Maudie... (SHE THROWS HER ARMS AROUND MAUDIE AND BEGINS TO CRY) I wouldn't do owt to hurt thee, lass. Honest. I love thee. I do. I just forget. I forget what I do with things. And these teeth. These new teeth don't fit right. I'm in pain, Maudie, all the time. I swear it.

MAUDIE: I know. I know. You've just got to wear them, then they'll get better. (SHE KISSES ALICE'S FOREHEAD AND GENTLY PRISES THE EXERCISE BOOK OUT OF ALICE'S HAND) I know you forget things, mam. Come on, now. It's time to get your things together.

LIGHTS DIM. MUSIC: TOTAL ECLIPSE OF THE HEART BY BONNIE TYLER. AS MUSIC FADES, SPOTLIGHT COMES UP ON HOSPITAL BED WITH SMALL LOCKER NEXT TO IT AND SOME *GET WELL SOON* CARDS ON TOP OF THE LOCKER. ALICE, IN A NIGHTDRESS, IS BEING HELPED INTO BED BY THE SISTER

SISTER: There, there, that's better.

ENTER MAUDIE

SISTER: And look - your daughter's come to see you. Isn't that nice now? I know I'm leaving you in good hands. (EXIT SISTER)

MAUDIE: Hello, mam. I told you I'd be back. I told you not to worry. They told me you've been out shopping. The sister says you used real money.

ALICE: What's the use of real money when they don't let you buy what you want? I wanted sweets. I love sweets. You know I love sweets, Maudie. Lollies. Barley sugars. Chocolate buttons. Thee and me's got no secrets. I told 'em we'd pay us way like we allus do. But they won't let me buy sweets.

MAUDIE: Going shopping keeps you in touch, mam. Keeps your mind active. Stops you forgetting.

ALICE: (ANGRY) I don't forget! You're the one that forgets!

MAUDIE: Here, I've brought you some more Get Well Soon cards. There's one from Jeanie, Dot's friend. That was nice of her, wasn't it? And there's one from Joe Maynard, Arthur's friend when they worked at Forgemasters. I think that Joe must fancy you.

ALICE: Joe? I don't remember a Joe.

MAUDIE: It's a nice card. They're both nice. I'll put them up for you. (MAUDIE GOES OVER TO LOCKER)

ALICE: Thee's my angel, Maudie. Thee's my little angel. Like the little angels on the ceiling.

MAUDIE: And you're my *big* angel, mam. My Blue Angel, like Marlene Dietrich.

ALICE: Ay, people said I looked like her. Like a film star.

MAUDIE: They were right.

ALICE: Who's this Joe? Joe who? (PAUSE) You don't hold it against me, do you? About Barry? You don't...?

MAUDIE: No, mam. It's forgotten.

ALICE: (SUDDENLY SUSPICIOUS) Are you still seeing him?

MAUDIE: No, mam, I'm *not* still seeing him. Not for years. And years. Honest. It's so long ago. You forget...

ALICE: I don't forget! I'm not the one that forgets! *You* forget! You're forgetting one thing now! I know about you!

MAUDIE: Shush, mam, don't be silly.

ALICE: Oh, but I do! Oh I do, I do! Oh yes, I do!

MAUDIE: Course you do. You know me. I'm Maudie. But you don't want to shout. The nurses don't like it.

ALICE: I know all about you – tellin' people I'm going funny in the head. Your own mother. Oh, they listen to you because you're lah-di-dah. That's why they put me in here. Then you come in, straight-faced, bringing me your bloody cards! I don't want your bloody cards!

ALICE LASHES OUT, KNOCKS THE CARDS OFF THE LOCKER TOP AND LAUGHS

ALICE: But I can see through it, through all your airs an' graces, young lady. An' I know why you do it, don't think I don't know!

MAUDIE: (DISTRAUGHT, PICKING UP THE CARDS) Oh mam, don't! It's because you're ill, mam, that's why you talk this way. You know you are. I love you!

ALICE: I've always had one thing you've not had, and you don't like that. It eats away at you. Tha thinks I don't see it, lass, but I do. You never knew your grandad. Oh, such a man he was! When our mam died, there was just the three of us then. Albert and me and your grandad. And he never needed another woman, never needed to bring another woman back. *I* saw to that!

MAUDIE: (ALARMED) Mam, what are you saying? You don't know what you're saying.

ALICE: Oh, you hate me! I can see it! Else you wouldn't leave me in here.

MAUDIE: We're going home. Honest. Soon. Saturday.

ALICE: I don't know why I'm in here. I can understand with some of 'em. Two bricks short of a load, some of 'em are. And they smell, Maudie!

MAUDIE: I know, mam, you've told me.

ALICE: They smell! I'll start smelling like that if I have to stay here, I know I will.

MAUDIE: They wouldn't have you in here if you weren't ill, mam. You'll be home soon, I promise.

ALICE: Oh, wouldn't they? I know why it is! It's 'cause of him, isn't it?

MAUDIE: I love you, mam. You're all I've got.

ALICE: You've had it on your mind all these years an' I don't care who knows it. Oh, I should've known, I should've known when Albert left the house to you instead of me. You made Albert think I was funny in the head then, didn't you? You worked your wiles on him and he couldn't see through you. All these years!

MAUDIE: It's your house too. It'll always be yours as much as it's mine. Please...

ALICE: I won't shush. I don't care who hears! (SHE LOOKS ROUND, RELISHING THE MOMENT)

MAUDIE: I'll bring you a cup of tea. Would you like that?

ALICE: I don't want cups of tea. I don't want nowt from the likes of thee. You've always 'ated me!

MAUDIE: It's not true!

ALICE: So now you think you're rid of me!

MAUDIE: No, mam, you'll be home soon. You an' me. Like it always was. I'll look after you.

ALICE: You? Look after me? Who d'you think you are then? You've never had what I had! Never had the looks! Never had the men comin' round you like I had! No, never! And it's because of *him*, isn't it? You've never forgiven me!

MAUDIE: Yes I have, mam. You were right. He'd never have got that divorce. He was stringing me along. There, I've said it. (BEAT) I start to read those letters now and I think: What a fool I must've been! You're right – I never could get the men, could I? That's why I keep them, the letters. To remind me to be sensible. You were right about Barry. I know that now.

ALICE: (CONFUSED) Barry? Barry? Don't play innocent with me, my girl. Don't give me Barry. Who's this Barry?

MAUDIE: Mam...You know. Barry. My fancy man. The letters.

ALICE: You always wanted 'im. Always comin' down in that bloody nightdress, showin' all you've got. Call that decent? Well, *I* don't! 'E was the only one, the only one out of all of them that was a real man, the only man as could hold a candle to your grandad. Oh, I knew what was goin' on though. I knew you wanted 'im. What was 'e to do? 'E was a man with a man's feelings. And then he was gone, slung 'is 'ook like the rest. *My Cyril*! And there you were, with your sly ways. Lucky cards. Lucky cards, Uncle Cyril! I'll touch them, Uncle Cyril, I'll touch the lucky cards. Touch them like I'd touch a lad I was courting! All soft and loving and gentle like! I saw you! (WHILE SHE IS SPEAKING SHE REACHES OUT AND TAKES SOME OF THE *GET WELL SOON* CARDS FROM MAUDIE'S HAND AND RUBS THEM SUGGESTIVELY ACROSS MAUDIE'S CHEEK) But *I* was the one he wanted – not you! An' you've never forgiven me!

MAUDIE: (SUDDENLY HYSTERICAL, THROWING THE CARDS ALL OVER THE ROOM) Aaaaaaaaaarrrgghhh!!!

THEN SILENCE. MAUDIE LOOKS ROUND, GUILTY, AMAZED AT HER OWN VIOLENCE

MAUDIE: (QUIETLY) I'll get that cup of tea. I'll get it now.

ALICE : (SHOUTING) I'll never forgive thee!

MAUDIE: I'll get you that cup of tea.

MAUDIE MOVES OFF, SLOWLY, PAINFULLY,
OUT OF THE LIGHT

ALICE : (SHOUTING NOW) It's dishonest and I hate
dishonesty! I'll never forgive thee!

LIGHTS DIM AS ALICE'S VOICE RISES TO A
CRESCENDO

ALICE: Ever since you were small! It's been thee and
me, the two of us. You know how much I love my home.
Our home. I do. I don't like bein' away. I don't like being
'ere! In this bed. In this 'ospital. I don't! Take me home,
Maudie!

LIGHTS GO OUT ON BED, UP ON SETTEE

MAUDIE: (SITTING ON SETTEE, TALKING INTO
PHONE) I can't help it, Dot. I've made up my mind.
Allright. I've *changed* my mind. (PAUSE) I don't know
if she'll be happy. But I don't think she'd be happy back
here, with me. I don't think she *can* be happy. Never.
Not now. (BEAT) They don't call them loony bins, Dot.
Not these days. I don't think they ever did. They're just..
well, places. Places where they take people like mam.
Where they can look after her. (PAUSE) I've got to have
a life of my own.(BEAT) *Life*. Four letters. Opposite of
death. (BEAT) Even now. Yes, I know I'm sixty-three.

Yes, I do feel guilty. *Guilty*. Six letters. Blameworthy, culpable, wicked. I'll have to live with it. For the rest of my life. (BEAT) *Rest*. Four letters. remainder. Leftover. Rest in peace. Goodbye, Dot.

SHE PUTS DOWN THE PHONE, PICKS UP PAPER WITH CROSSWORD, SPEAKS CALMLY NOW

MAUDIE: Five down. Anger of king in far time. Seven letters. I've already got the R. Easy. R for Rex, out is far, age is time. *Outrage*. (SHE PUTS DOWN PAPER, STANDS UP, FACES AUDIENCE) All alone. By the telephone. You are my sunshine, my only sunshine. That old black magic's got me in its spell... Oh such a man you were! Oh how she loved you! (BEAT) *Love*. Four letters. Affection. Devotion. Strong attachment to one of the opposite sex. (PAUSE) *Love*. Four letters. Tennis score. Zero. Nothing. Nil. (PAUSE) *Home*. Four letters. Never away. House. (PAUSE) Home. Institution. Loony bin. (PAUSE) *Home*. Four letters. Song title. When shadows fall and trees whisper day is ending. Home sweet home. Home alone. Home is where the heart is. (BEAT) Home at last.

LIGHTS GO DOWN. COMPLETE DARKNESS.
MUSIC: HOLDING BACK THE YEARS BY SIMPLY
RED.

END

Nettle Books: More drama by Michael Yates

The Bronte Boy

Young Branwell Bronte, who once ruled an imaginary world, is now a man, grown mad trying to cope with the real one. Having failed as a poet and painter, as doomed in love as he is in literature, he slips ever more quickly down the road of drink, drugs and despair. His loving father Patrick and talented sister Charlotte fight a last-ditch stand for his salvation, but it is Branwell's sinister friend, gravedigger John Brown, who threatens to have the last word in this ultimately terrifying take on the brilliant family we have read so much about and all thought we knew so well.
Paperback. **ISBN** 978-0-9561513-1-5. **£6**

QWERTYUIOP

It's the age of Britain's first woman prime minister – but not *every* female feels the surge of power. A group of unemployed Yorkshire women on a cut-price typing course speak their minds about men, politics, men, work, men, sex, men and each other – with catastrophe effects!
Paperback. **ISBN** 978-0-9933729-1-9   **£6**.

Nettle Books: Novels, Stories, Poetry

Heaven Scent

John Winter
A comic novel set in the swinging sixties. Charlie wanted to be part of the sexual revolution but it sort of passed him by. Now he and fellow reporters on a seaside weekly paper have something to take their minds off summers of love – when the sleepy resort is rocked by mystery explosions.
Paperback. **ISBN**:978-0-9561513-6-0   **£10**

Pomfret

Edited by Brian Lewis
Ten stories about historical Yorkshire town Pontefract by Yorkshire writers including Colin Hollis, Howard Frost, Linda Jones, Robin Gledhill, Ann Rhodes, Walter Storey and Susan McCartney. Illustrated by Yorkshire artists including Jane Walsh and Barbara Smith.
Paperback. **ISBN**: 978-0-9561513-8-4   **£8**

Scop

Helen Shay
Poems that provide revelation in a wide spectrum of styles from Biblical to rap. Char March says: "Enjoy her breadth of field on the world, her use of language and her great sense of humour."
Paperback. **ISBN** 978-0-9933729-2-6   **£7**

Nettle Books: Autobiography

Flying with a Broken Wing

Sat Mehta
A boy's story of growing up in India's turbulent
times. Sat Mehta was five years old when he and
his family became destitute refugees, his uncle
murdered during partition riots. Then Sat suffered a
broken arm, and amputation seemed inevitable.
Then a visiting English surgeon offered him a
lifeline...
Paperback. **ISBN**:978-0-9561513-2-2   **£10**